John Huntley Skrine

Columba

A Drama

John Huntley Skrine

Columba
A Drama

ISBN/EAN: 9783337342111

Printed in Europe, USA, Canada, Australia, Japan

Cover: Foto ©Andreas Hilbeck / pixelio.de

More available books at **www.hansebooks.com**

COLUMBA

A DRAMA

BY

JOHN HUNTLEY SKRINE

WARDEN OF GLENALMOND
AUTHOR OF 'A MEMORY OF EDWARD THRING'

WILLIAM BLACKWOOD AND SONS
EDINBURGH AND LONDON
MDCCCXCIII

DEAR listener of the tale half-told,
  Whose singer's breath was breath from thee ;
If to the spirits' guarded fold
  A voice of kin find pathway free,
If memories of a music old
  Live on with her who bade it be,—
O then, beyond this beat of time,
Love yet is listener of the rhyme.

COLUMBA, who was also called Columcille—that is, Dove of the Cell —came on both sides of the blood-royal of Ireland : for his father, Fedhlimidh, was of the northern Hy Neill, and his mother, Eithné, had for ancestor Cathair Mor, the first king of Leinster, afterwards king of Ireland. In youth he became a monk, and presently a founder of churches and monasteries, whereof the first was Derry and the greatest Durrow. Yet, when he was now forty years old, having a quarrel with Diarmid, king of all Ireland, concerning the slaying, when in sanctuary, of Curnan, son of the king of Connaught, Columba roused to war his own clansmen and set them against Diarmid, whom they overthrew with great slaughter of his Meath-men. In sorrow for this bloodshed, and at the bidding of Molasius, abbot of Inishmurry, Columba set out for Scotland, to convert the Picts to Christ, and so atone for his wrong-doing. He sailed at Whitsuntide in the year of Christ 563, and the forty-second of his own age, with twelve companions, and settled on the island of Hy, that is now called Iona. There they built a monastery, and from it they went out to preach in all Pictland. Afterwards there arose a dispute between Aedh, king of Ireland, and Aidan, king of Dalriada in Scotland. Now Aidan had been consecrated king by Columba, and was his friend. So Columba went with Aidan to Ireland to meet Aedh and the Irish chiefs at the Synod called of Drumceit. There did the abbot cause Aedh both to free the Dalriad people from subjection, and also to recall a decree by which he would have driven the bards from his kingdom. From Ireland came Columba back to Hy, and after many good works there died, nigh seven-and-seventy years old, in the year of Christ 597, and was buried by his own monks alone. For a great wind arose straightway upon his passing, and blew for three days and nights, so that no boat could cross the sound to reach the island ; but when the burial was fully ended, forthwith the wind fell and the seas grew calm.

DRAMATIS PERSONÆ.

COLUMBA, Abbot of Iona.

BAITHEN,
ERNAN,
FECHNO,
MOCHONNA,
} Monks.

DIORMIT, a young Monk, Attendant on Columba.

RONAN, a Bard.

FERGUS, an Irish Chief, Kinsman of Columba.

MOLASIUS, a Hermit, Soul's-friend (Confessor) to Columba.

A Retainer of Fergus.

A Dalriad.

COLUMBA.

————◆————

ACT FIRST.

SCENE I.

The Monastery at Derry. A.D. 561. BAITHEN *and* ERNAN *seated.*

BAITHEN.

How heavy, Ernan, is this waiting time !
Ere now there should be news.   A week ago
The clans were up.

ERNAN.

   Yes, and our Abbot there.
Men loiter not where he is.

BAITHEN.

    I should know it,
Who followed with him when he roused the chiefs.

A

They are hot enough, when fight is forward, they;
But he was fire, at council or in field
A hovering flame still at their backs to scorch
Doubter or lingerer.   O to see him stand
That eve among the clansmen when the chiefs
Besought his blessing!   On a little mound
He rose; the mustered spears before his breast
Bristled; I watched him o'er them.   Head uncowled
For heat, and liker knight unhelmeted
Than churchman, tall he towered, his lifted hand
Beckoning kinglike: then the voice rolled out:
—Ah! but we know the voice of him, so large
It fills the wide air as the thunder fills,
Yet the clear syllables in a stealing rain
Chime on the senses pure and musical:
So deep, it girds you like a grappling wave,
And sways the stoutest-footed down the tide.
O when he spoke of vengeance, Curnan dragged
From sanctuary of the great Abbot's arms,
The fair boy's blood dashed on the sacred skirts,
A shiver ran across the glancing field
Of spear-heads, and there heaved a passionate sob
Of wrath that would have roared in storm, but he,
Spreading his palms, as who would still the seas
By miracle, overawed them to a hush;

So blessed their arms and them, and let them go.
Was ever holy man so royal as he?

ERNAN.

Less royal were more holy.   Ay; 'uncowled.'
Somewhat too loose our Abbot wears the cowl
To my poor thinking, dare I speak my thought.
These knightly warrings and these kingly ways,
I cannot like them.   We are men of peace.
Who takes the sword shall perish by the sword.

BAITHEN.

He takes no sword.   You wrong him.   He but guides,
In this high quarrel of avenging God,
The earthlier arm that takes it.

ERNAN.
                              Yes, I know.
Yet I do fear his saintliness may draw
A soil from this hot traffic with the world.
For who can pray aright whose veins are swelled
With anger, or with fierce expectancy
Of bloody news, or, haply, sights of blood?
These trampling musters and harsh horns of war
Will put him from his prayers.

BAITHEN.

That will they not.
Brother, you never were Columba's man;
You know him not.   But I remember how
That self-same night, late in the second watch,
I rose, for sleep I could not, and would pace
The moonlight glades awhile; but there I heard
A rustle in the brake, and came on him
Risen to his feet, but praying still, as one
Drawn from the earth by energy of the prayer.
Uppillared in the lonely beam he stood:
And by wrung lip and ghost-white cheek I read
Sign of a fading agony in the face.
I heard him murmur Curnan's name, and knew
He pleaded for his peace, with such a tone,
So yearningly beseeching and so rapt
With holy passion, that all shamed I hid
And stole away over the silent moss,
Unnoted.   But that white face follows me.
O he is saint for all his kingliness!

ERNAN.

And well and warmly have you pleaded it,
Good brother: saintly is he: I were churl
To question it; and yet—and yet, my fears

Root deep (God grant them vain !) that he will rue
His commerce with the men of feud and fray.

            [RONAN *the bard is heard singing outside.*

O the Dove of the Cell hath the Eagle for kin.
When the banner is blown, when the bugles begin . . .

BAITHEN.

The voice of Ronan, as I live !   He brings
The news of battle.

    (*To* RONAN *entering.*)   Speak ! is it well, is it well ?

RONAN.

Should I come singing, if my news were ill ?
The men of Meath are flying on all the hills.
Columba is avenged.

BAITHEN.

    Now praised be God !

RONAN.

There lie three thousand stark among the brakes
Of Meathmen, and stout fellows of our own
A scant five hundred, but too many so.

ERNAN.

Three thousand lives for one ! a goodly toll.

And half a thousand more in taking it.
Will God make reckoning for trangression thus ?

BAITHEN.

More, more, good Ronan.   Tell us all, and how
Columba did, and where ye fought.

RONAN.
                                        We fought
Hard by Drumcliff.   The Brethren of that House
Were on the hills to watch us,—would have fought,
A score of them : Columba drove them back.
' What should they do with fighting ?   Let them pray.'
Yet monks there fought too in our battle ranks,
Some three or four.   Our scouts had found the king
Couched in our path among the matted hills
That hide Culdrevny, scarce a league away,
And we should rush upon him with the morn.
Then under the last stars Columba came
Along the ranks to bless them : tall he stood
Between the torches : pale of cheer was he
With vigil on the ghostly moor, but pale
As with the white fires of a stormy dawn.
Some said that, as he blessed us, very fire
Was sprayed from waving sleeve and moving hand,
Most wonderful, and like the fluttering heat
That fumes from summer meads.   I know not this.

But silent-footed as a troop of elves
The army moved. Dun hollow and dun height
Grew greyer, and not yet the mist had risen,
When far to right a watcher cried, and far
To left the alarum bickered down their line,
And all the hill was live with starting foes,
And roaring open war we bounded on them.
I had lost the Master in the march, but came
Upon him in the fight. Beside an oak
He leaned, his left hand stayed upon a bough,
The other clenched as if a hilt were in it.
The trenchant eyes under a knotted brow
Seemed to see all things in the swarming field,
But saw not me. 'Father,' I cried, 'you press
Too near the vanguard's skirt.' He answered not,
Nor cast a look upon me. To and fro,
With rush and flight and rally and staggering shock,
Across blind copses of the bellowing dells
Tumbled the unsteady battle, till I cried,
Quailing, 'Good Master, shall we win it?' He
Answered me not. A random spear-point fell
Glancing the oak-trunk. 'Master, shelter you,'
I groaned in agony. But he answered not,
Nor looked, nor stirred. Only the even breath
Through the stretched nostril labouringly toiled.
But on a sudden he put hand to ear

And hearkened, flushing; and I too could hear,
Through the thick uproar, hoarse a slughorn blare
A point of onset. 'Twixt the teeth he muttered,
' He is o'er the moss, he has turned their right, good Fergus ;
We have them—as I told him.' Then he fell
To the old mute stare again. My throbbing heart
Had told three hundred, when he cried aloud,
' That stir on the far hillock yonder—see,
Canst thou not see it, bard ?' I saw it not.
But on the instant rose the angry wail
Of men borne hopeless back, and in the air
Hung, till our peal of victory swallowed it,
And all one way the heavy battle swung.
Then under it the torn brake bent again,
And snapped with rushing footsteps ; up the slope
Billowed the chase of war, and on the brow,
A moment poising, stretched a vulture wing,
Flecking the sky with banner and stormy spear,
Then stooped upon the fliers that fight no more.

   Thereon the mighty Abbot turned his eyes,
And with their large smile all enfolding me,
Said, ' Here is goodly news, my bard, for Derry.
And men will hear to-morrow (will they not ?)
A battle psalm of our sweet singer tell
How fought the stars against Columba's wrong.'
   Yea, will ye hear it ?

BAITHEN.

Blithely, Ronan.

ERNAN.

Bard,

Knew you those three or four who fought, you said,
Against Columba's bidding?

RONAN.

Nay, I know not.

Or—how should I forget him?—one I knew
Through all his war-gear: and he whispered me
Be silent.   But his name—how call you him?
The comely boy with the black eyes and hot,
Free spirit, him who took his vows with us
Seven months ago.

ERNAN.

Mochonna?

RONAN.

Yea, the same.

The Abbot's godson, or I err.

ERNAN.

Mochonna!
I would you had said some other.

RONAN.

Nay, 'twas he.
But friends, my harp's afret to tell the tale
Her fashion.   Listen.
(*Sings.*)
Faint of tread as mists on moorland trooping,
Linking wavering hand in hand, and looping
Fold on cloudy fold,—
Faint of tread our hunters o'er the wold
Come with holden breath and helmet stooping,
Lest the night reveal
Tramplings of the Neil,
Lest the trembling heath
Warn the men of Meath
Connaught's sword upon their sleep is swooping.

Hark!
What was it there?
Foeman's signal, or owl's
Hoot in the brake?
Mark!

Comrade, the hazels shake.

Was it a hare

Starting, a fox that prowls?

No, in a trice

Ere an eyelid's fall or a heart's beat twice,

To left and to right

With a cry running ever before it in widening peal,

As a wind on the wheat, as a fire on the fern, the quick
furrow of fight

Sunders the ridges of steel.

Shock of the mighty, reel

Of the helmet under the sword,

Wrestle of spear and spear,

Rattle of mail on the sward.

Fire of the battle, and fear:

Fear that to fire will spring

At the stormy veer of the soul,

And ride o'er the war's uproll

On the glory of danger's wing.

Who is this arisen to rule us, loftier than our lords of fray?

Who is this all still in tumult, all aflame in our dismay?

Hood for helm: for mail a girdle. Shines not in his hand
the sword.

With the light of eyes he smiteth, and he routeth with the
word.

Whom we knew not, lo! we know him, now in danger's
    burning hour,
Him who walks the fire and burns not, armoured with
    the nameless power;
Him whose ears have heard the High One's counsel; who
    the warcraft knows
Of the secret lightnings raining viewless ruin o'er the
    foes.
Lo! the Dove, that of the dove name bears the pureness,
    not the fear:
Lo! the Dove, that hath the eagle for his kinsman and
    his peer:
Blenched not he, nor plume he ruffled when the battle-
    horns began,
On our standard-beam alit and steadfast in the reeling van.
Who shall fright him, who shall front him, who shall
    countercharm the spell
Of the Dove from out the eyrie, of the soldier from the
    cell?

Harp of glory,
Raise the wail:
Teach, O harp, thy strings to tell of woe!
Tell of those who chant not with our chanting,
Brother hearts, that bled to make our vaunting;
And they linger where they drave the foe.

Sing we sorrow o'er the proud, fair faces,
Starward staring;
O'er the strong limbs couched in heathy places
Frorely faring.
Cold they lie, whose souls a moment burning
Flamed away:
Cold they lie, and wait an unreturning
Beam of day.
Who are these, like mists in moonlight trooping,
Fold on fold and hand in hand enlooping,
Light as breath, and white as death, on moorland
hoar?
These the shades are of our brothers parted,
Empty shadows of our mighty-hearted:
They will meet us, but they greet us nevermore.

[*Seeing them gone.*

What! gone? and let me sing to the bare walls,
Ay, and bare table (hunger pinch them for't!),
Nor offered the poor harper bite or sup.
Oh these lean men of God, the way of them!
'Tis better when the Master's here, he knows
A man who fasts may pray, but sing he cannot.
But what? We are soldiers; I'll go forage for it.

[*Exit.*

SCENE II.

A moor near the monastery of Derry.   At night.
COLUMBA *alone.*

COLUMBA.

By my much weariness the night is old.
Yet the dark lightens not.   Would it were day!
And yet not so: I would not day should rise
Upon a night outwatched so barrenly.
I have watched, but not to prayer.   Prayer from my soul
Withers away, as sleep from aching brows
The more we woo it.   Tender dews of heaven
Rain over the dark sod I kneeled on, rain
Large over all things else but only me,
Dry in the drenched field as a Gideon's fleece.
Pray can I not; and something ails my soul.

Nay, 'tis but Nature's use, a faintness bred
By strain of the tasked spirit; nothing more.
Have I not known it? after stormy day
Of fire and of anointing, when a truth
Burned in my heart and flamed on lip and caught
From edge to edge the pale, lit multitude,
How on the rapt hour fell a morrow blank

As grey March heavens where the east wind creeps,
So lightless, stark, and cold. 'Tis ever so.
The hand of Spirit's jealous sister, Flesh,
Prisons the dove-wings of her heavenly twin
Caught from their moment's flight.   And in this cause
Body and Soul as honest yoke-fellows
Have toiled and tired :—that rousing of the clans ;
Vigil and march and vigil ; an army's fate
Laid all on me ; and that soul-shaking fight,
And what befell me after with the dead !
Yea, 'tis but spendthrift Nature's hour of ebb.
A night of slumber brings again the flow.

Will it ?   I know not.   Something deeper ails
Than sleep can physic.
                                        Ha ! What stirred ? Who cries ?
Folly !   The night-jar's ruckle as he shifts
From brake to brake.   I start at nothings now.
It made me think upon the cries I heard
Through the drear darkness where our lanterns crept
Among the dying : fluttering cries of pain
That rose and drifted, rose and drifted thick
As multitudinous bleat of the shorn flock
At night in chill June meadows.   There was one
Lifted a warped face to the gleam, and cursed
Me and my quarrel.   Ah ! the stricken one,

He was past knowing me: but yet it hurts,
That dead man's curse. 'My quarrel.' Was it mine:
Not God's in His wronged justice? Yet he cursed.
And I must still remember that he cursed.

Just Heaven, I warred for Justice. Is the blame
Mine, if she bared so blind a sword, and mowed
A swathe of many to reach the guilty One?
For land, for pelf, for pride my tribesmen flock
Gaily to battle; nay, for battle's sake:
No better. I have taught them war for right.
The blood be on the wrongers, not on me.
Let Diarmid see to that. My hands are clean.

Yet the man cursed: and I must still remember.

A shiver pricks my flesh. It is the dawn.
Her cold forefinger touched me through the dark.
Yet night is solid everywhere. My flesh?
Nay, was it cold that pricked, or flesh that shrank?

My hands are clean; my hands——

Out, out, and out upon it! 'Tis not so.
I lie to my own soul. I am not clean.
It is my sin, O soul, it is my sin

Winged that sore arrow of his curse: my sin
Venomed its point with rancours.   Clean I am not:
Their blood is thick upon me, and I knew,
Dissembler! and I laboured not to know it.
But that lodged arrow galling all my side
Devours me: and I dared not, miserable!
Set hand and pluck the iron out, and brave
Agony of unsealed wound and spouting vein.
Dared not?   What is there else I dared not, I
Who on the roaring strand of battle felt
The sharp spray on my lips unshrinking?   Dare not?
'Twere ill then with Columba.   O my soul,
We have braved all else, shall we not brave my guilt?
Stand forth, my sin, and let me look on thee:
Forth from thy lair, full-statured as thou art,
Featured and limbed as the Ill Sire begot:
Stand armed, a traitor challenged; let me know thee
As warrior knows his foeman, point to point.

O Thou just God, thus have I done and thus.
There was a man of Thine, if Thine he was
For his much labour's sake, a youth who vowed
To teach the fiery hearts of our wild Erin
Burn for the Christ alone: a prince who cast
Hopes from him of a crown, red gold of earth,
So might he reach the starrier coronal

That brows a Prince with God.   For this he dwelt
Apart with visions, till the visions broke
In blossom and o'er-ran the jarring land
With shrines of peace and prayerful brotherhoods.
　　God! what is this has cut my path across?
What pit of horror opens at my feet,
Yawning, with blood of men that blackens in it
And fumes that mount and madden?   Is it I
Have done this deed,—I, that came preaching peace,
Have wrought confusion, brother's hand on brother,
And this red chrism of blood in hatred shed?
I, is it I have done it, I that dreamed
So purely—I, and not some other man?
I cannot think it mine: but that abhorred
Red gleam of blood once looked on fills my eyes,
And falls in blots before them where they fall,
And writes my guilt on air and field and sky,
'Shedder of blood, shedder of blood.'   O Christ,
Is all then fallen to this: the dream that blessed
My cradle, angels of the infancy,
And prophesyings that sealed me saint: to this
The fast, the prayer, the vigil, and the brows
That felt thy finger through the trembling dark
Descend in consecration,—fallen to this?
I hear the fierce kings mutter, 'Even as we
Is he, Columba: hates and wars and kills

After man's kind, no other; he that bade
Forbear, forgive. Ha! ha! he is wiser now:
Wise as his flock that live the olden way.'
O to have lived for sainthood, then to slay
The saint within me! Never more to me,
Pale with his violence when the flame-fit dies
Shall turn the vengeful clansman, 'Cleanse me, father,
For thou art pure.' Nor, lit with ghostly hopes,
The young boy lift his eyes and murmur, 'Master,
Thou hast the words of life: I serve with thee.
I shall not cleanse nor rule; the power is lost
I cleansed with, fallen my sceptre over men.
Men! is't with men I reckon? Holy God,
Thee, against Thee my sin is, Thine the face
That will not look on me, so cold a cloud,
Crimson with mists of blood that welter in it,
Curtains me out: and through the cloud I feel,
Unseen, Thy brows of judgment wintrily
Beat on my soul and bear it down to earth.
And dead as earth of earth my soul, but quick
With icy pangs of horror, and nameless pain
Of glory beheld and lost, and bliss not mine,
Cut off from the face of God, from the face of God.

SCENE III.

*The isle of Inishmurry. The monastery of Molasius
in the background.* COLUMBA *landing.*

COLUMBA.

Lo! Christ's last watch-tower in the West, the isle
Of wise Molasius and his anchorites.
The wave that splits upon this rock has heard
The talk of winds at the earth's margin, fresh
From the evening star; or in dumb bosom bears
From ocean gardens, where no shipman comes,
Charm-murmurs of the dread Hesperian witch,
And foams their echo first on shores of Christ.

    There peep the red domes of the hermit folk
Above the rampart, where they hive like bees,
But work not bee-like. Would I hive with these,
If he should bid? God knows.

    (*To* ATTENDANT.)   Go thou and say
Columba waits on wise Molasius,
To speak with him when leisure serves from prayer.

    To hive with these—a hermit? I could not, I.
To crawl from cell to shrine, from shrine to cell,
To crouch and muse in the close vault, to moan
Sad litanies to the unresponding wave;

Or when the demons wake the seas, and all
The deep isle labours in the surge, to feel
The unused, unwasted might within me pent
Rage at its chain to spend itself in storm;
Until the grey years dateless, deedless, dumb,
Chronicled only by the whitening beard,
Crumble to ash my manhood.   God! I will not.
Free air, free field, free service give me, room,—
Though but to bleed in or to die in, room.

> [MOLASIUS *enters.*

MOLASIUS.

God and all holy angels, son, be with thee.
Thou wouldst have speech with me.   I ask not why.
Our chapel—shall it serve us?

COLUMBA.

> Rather here,

Under these heavens, at the headland's edge.
I can speak better so.   The shower that dashed
My rowers' backs is overblown; the next
Pearls but the blue sky's edge with cloudy plumes.
An hour before its wing flap over us.

MOLASIUS.

So be it, son.

> [*They sit.*

COLUMBA.

Father, thou wouldst not ask
What brought me here; haply because thou knowest.

MOLASIUS.

We dwell afar, yet something reaches us.
Your wrath with Diarmid, and the woful field
Culdrevny, and that session of the Church
Which but for Brendan would have banned thee, this
Mochonna told us: he had fought himself,
Vowed monk although he be, for love of thee.
Alas! the wild blood in our churchman hearts
That preach peace, not ensue it.   Here he bides,
Sorrowing for that soul's peace his violence slew.

COLUMBA.

Mochonna!   Deep you pierce.   Mochonna, he
On whose babe-brow I traced the saving sign,
He, too, undone through me!   The boy I taught
His first Christ-lore, and saw his musing eyes
Deepen with young resolve, and loved him, he
Among the murdered souls whose blood I bear!
The slain men are at ease, their spirits rest
In pardon; Abban told me when he came
From prayer and from that angel whom he meets.

But, for the living souls whose peace I slew
That should have taught them peace, what penance,
  what——
Father, it was for this I sought thee out.
I have bent my knees in every holy shrine
Of Erin, questioned all our wisest, prayed
Nightlong by hallowed wells or under shade
Of secret oaks, where the white angels dwell;
But voice of man nor angel eased my pain.
Last, 'I will seek Molasius,' I cried,
'The soul's-friend of my boyhood, first and best.
Far from our jars among pure seas he dwells,
He prays in the great silences, he hears
God's voice across the storms, 'tis he shall name
The penance-doom that makes Columba clean.'
Speak.   By thy sentence I have vowed to stand.
Father, upon my knees I wait it: speak.

MOLASIUS.

I cannot speak the penance that makes clean;
For, son, I know not any.

COLUMBA.

   Thou, not thou?

MOLASIUS.

Not I, nor any. Thou hast asked amiss.
What penance did the Christ who cleansed us all ?
Death ?   But He died I think as warriors die,
Who choose the pain for mastery's sake, the death
Because the victory comes no otherwise.
But pain, by use unblessed, how should it heal ?

COLUMBA.

Strange words from such as thou, whose very life
Seems pain, in prison on this mournful isle.

MOLASIUS.

In prison !   I was never free but here.
Bound; but the great God's visions are not bound;
Bound, north and south and east, but upwards free
From lone rock up to highest heaven of heavens.
My doom be mine who know it.   Other thine.
See here the sinewed hand that lies in mine,
The keen eyes under the great brow, the frame
And stature, auguries of toil and rule.
The toil, the rule must be thy penance, son.
Go work for Christ, go work.

COLUMBA.

> Ha! sayest thou so?

MOLASIUS.

Go work, His shepherd on the hillside, keep
Thy vigils by the fold, and let the frost
Of night, the noonday's drought consume thee; bring
Through gusts upon the giddy mountain stair
The strayed lamb home; and, for thy penance, bleed
Grappling the fanged wolf in his ravin heat,
Thy blood for theirs. For every soul thy wrath
Sent to God's judgment-seat unshriven, bring
A hundred to His fold. Lo! I Molasius
Pronounce the sentence. Yet not I but Christ.

COLUMBA (*starting to his feet*).

O earth and heaven, heaven and wide earth! Is this
Thy sentence, this? Father, my dear heart's wish
Had chosen as thou bidst. To toil, to dare,
War with the wolf, to range the stirring field
Shepherd and fighter—O my very dream!
What, can man's wishing be God's willing, joy
Be penance, and the chastening cup of gall
Run in my veins a cordial? Can it be?

D

Sweet justicer, art wise as thou are sweet?
Can that please heaven which pleases flesh so well?

MOLASIUS.

Fair son, and hath not God, then, made the flesh?
And sown the strength in't, and delight of strength,
And longing for the battle? He who taught
The erne his sunward circlings, gave withal
The thrills and rapture of the unpractised wing
That prick his strong youth skyward. Doubt me not.
Man's nature is God's oracle, and grace
Is to know nature as God made her first.
But, O young brother mine, mistrust not yet
Thy doom for over-sweetness! Hear the rest.
But stoop and let me speak it in thy ear.
I have no heart except to whisper it.

[He whispers.

COLUMBA.

' No more to Erin, never again to Erin!'
Unsay it, father.

MOLASIUS.

Nay, for I have said.
Thou must go labour for the heathen Pict,
And never come to Erin any more.

Such doom pronounce I, not the Lord but I :
But deem I have God's spirit uttering it.

COLUMBA.

Never to Erin again, never to Erin !

MOLASIUS.

Never again.   The crimson rain, that drenched
Culdrevny's sod, hath watered weeds too many.
In that red glebe shalt thou no harvest plant,
Gather no sheaves into thy bosom.   Tare
And spurge and poison-plant and mandrake choke
A ground for thy sake barren, and unblest
Harsh fallows, furrowed once by ploughs of war.
Ye cannot sow the strife and reap the peace.
Ah ! no.   Away, away: the ghosts would start
Thick from those trampled fields to shake thy prayer
With horror or heat: amid thy listening flock
Would faction's hell-hounds bay thy preaching dumb ;
Or the pale blood-feud's Fury, mocking, point
A gaunt forefinger at thy sullied robe
And shame the pleading saint.   It may not be.
Go.   Alba waits across the eastern sea,
White Alba, virgin of thy violences ;
Yea, white for harvest are the fields thereof.

COLUMBA.

But never more to come to Erin! Father,
Cloistered a life long on this naked rock,
With naked skies for all thy country, thou
Hast half forgot thy Erin. Seed of hers
Am I, and wither in an alien soil.
O great are birth and use! I am one half I,
Half her that nursed me, and my powers would faint
Unbuoyed on that strong river of her love,
Unwafted by her glory as a wind.
How should I teach the Christ to outland men,
Unknowing and unknown, dumb to the deaf,
Their spirits locked from mine? But Erin's heart
Was to my voice as is a minstrel's harp,
Familiar to his touch; for when he plays
Hand wakens harp, and harp awakens hand,
Live string, live finger wedded, and there grows
Music, of neither made, of twain begot.
He cannot harp aright on stranger chords, ·
Nor I make music sundered from my kin.

MOLASIUS.

Yea, great are birth and use and land and kin.
But when the Lord in Jewry walked, He owned
No kin but whoso wrought the Father's will,

Nor land so much as rests a weary head.
But God will give thee homes a hundredfold,
And God is able of rude Alba's stones
To raise up kin for thee.   Thy fears are blind,
The trick of use and 'wont.   What is, thou seest;
What shall be, canst not see.   Be strong and go.

COLUMBA.

My heart is broken in my breast.   I go,
Honouring thy word and my own vow.   I take
Thy counsel not thy comfort.   But I go.
And bless me thou who nevermore shalt bless.

[Kneels.

MOLASIUS (laying his hands on him).

The blessing of the God of Abraham,
Who calls His saints from country and from kin
Unto the land which He will show them, go
Before thee, and His promise comfort thee,
And make thy seed in number as the sand,
And thy soul's-children as the stars of heaven.

ACT SECOND.

SCENE I.

On the shore of Lough Foyle near the Monastery of Derry. A.D. 563.

FECHNO.

Baithen, the Abbot tarries long.

BAITHEN.

                    Let be.
He bides in yonder dingle, where the brook
Girdles a lawn about the Angel Oak,
Taking last leave of home : and partings seem
Ever too soon.   Are all the brethren here ?

FECHNO.

All, and not all.   All, but who has not come
Nor will come.

BAITHEN.

Who is he ?

FECHNO.

What, know you not
That Dallan goes not with us to the work,
But treads even now the road to Durrow ?

BAITHEN.

How !

And has Columba suffered it ?

FECHNO.

Ay, has he.
Truth, when the craven spoke, his brow grew big
With storm, but sudden all the gathered face
Fell back in utter sadness, and he sighed ;
' Ay, so: go back.   Better be Mark to-day
Than Judas on the morrow.   Go in peace !'
And Dallan went, but not in peace.   Ashamed
He stumbled some ten paces, turned, beheld,
Stern-sorrowful as the angel Adam saw
Posted by Eden Gate, Columba stand
Watching him.   Half I thought he would have run

And caught his knees, prayed pardon and return;
But eyes he dropped, shivered, and went his way.

BAITHEN.

And breaks our goodly Order of the Twelve,
And daunts our voyage with the omen.   Well,
Twelve were they once in Galilee, and one—
But we that are true men, aboard! and part
The oars between us: slack yon hawser's knot,
And half-mast high hoist up the sail, to lose
No minute when the Abbot crosses plank.
Fair sets the tide seaward, if fair can be
That bears us out from Erin.   Friends, aboard!

———

SCENE II.

The oak-grove at Derry.   COLUMBA *alone.*

COLUMBA.

How otherwise, than as I feared, the end
Has fallen at last.   I thought to break away
With such a horror of life-sundering pain
As rends the live-root mandrake.   'Tis not so.
The bitterness of death is past: the life
Born in the pang.   A promise vast and veiled,

A pillared flame uplift beyond the seas,
Beckons, and strains my heart until I go.
As one who treads some dreadful brink will leap
In fear's impatience to the death he fears,
So from this brink of home, this tottering verge
Of things which were my being, into the void,
Into the void, not to the death, I spring
Safe to the outspread eagle-wings of God.
They will uphold; I shall not die but live.
Not die.   But O fair mother, all-beloved
Erin, my nature's nurse, 'tis death to part!
Christ's soldier am I, but thy child: and all
The child within the man cries out for thee,
And catches clinging to thy skirts, and quails
To be torn away.   Yet will Columba go,
Though death it be.   O tender lap of earth,
And dewy meadows under glooming oaks,
And secret thickets of the chiding merle,
And ever-talking waters,—evermore
Farewell, and from a bleeding heart, farewell!
Farewell! Columba looks his last on Erin.

               [*Turns and sees* MOCHONNA.

Mochonna! in God's name what do you here?

MOCHONNA.

What should I do but seek my father?

E

COLUMBA.

Nay,

Too well of old you sought him.   But the Isle,
How came you from it ?   Did Molasius bid ?

MOCHONNA.

Nor bade, nor suffered, though I prayed him long.
I have broken pale.

COLUMBA.

Alas, a second time !

MOCHONNA.

Father, there came a fisher to the isle
One even, brought us news Columba's bark
Should sail for Alba ere this moon were full.
Mad was I that Molasius hindered me.
At night I rose, crept to the fisher's boat,
And hid me in the gear, until with dawn
He woke, the breeze being landward, and would go.
Him I persuaded, and the bird was flown,
No cageling gladlier.   Then by path or wild,
With sunrise and with moonrise, grudging sleep
Its hour of darkness, on I toiled to thee,
And find thee.   Father, make me of the Band.

COLUMBA.

Too hotly done, as ever. Was it well
To o'erleap the bound, against Molasius' word
Thy wise soul's friend and true ?

MOCHONNA.

Soul's friend have I
None other than Columba.

COLUMBA.

Nay, but hearken.
I loved thee, son, and loved thee to thy harm.
My path of blood dipped-in Mochonna, soiled
His virgin soul of peace, made riot there
Red dreams of wrath and horror, ghosts of guilt
That never will be wholly laid again,
Howe'er thy penance cleanse. This did my love.
Seek me not, boy, but fly : thy bane am I.

MOCHONNA.

Hearken me too, my father. Thou art bound
Hence to the Christless folk, to make them Christ's.
Yea, but a folk ungentle, men that slay
The stranger as we slay the beast ; untaught,
Untamed,—and thou wilt tame them. Ay, but how ?

Father, among the reddened heathen spears
I see thee quit thy trespass, blood with blood,
And purge thy violence in their violences.
And therefore, even therefore must I go.
With thee I sinned, let me be sained with thee,
Partake thy penance. Did thy path of blood `
Dip-in Mochonna? Let Mochonna wash
In the same purging stream. Hast made me sinner?
Then let me drink thy cup, endure thy chrism,
In the red martyrdom made saint with thee.

COLUMBA.

Boy, boy, thy passion tears me at the heart.
Yet must I teach it, make thy passion wise.
Bethink thee, thou art young, thy life unmaimed;
Wearing a scar, but whole. My life is broken,
A tree stem-severed, not to blossom more
Here in the soil of home, though God elsewhere
May graft it and give fruit. But thine is Erin
To grow in and abound and quite forget
This blight of fury on thy spring. Abide,
Live thy own life, nor lean on mine; be free;
Gather thy companies of holy men;
Bear rule, for thou art royal, be great for Christ.
Thou wilt not, no? Thou wilt not? Then for *me*
Abide. Behold me, how I need an heir.

I leave my plough in furrow, guide it thou;
My work is fallen, save thou rear it up;
My flock will faint, except thou shepherd it.
Then work my work, see what I saw not, be
Columba's soul in Erin. I shall walk
In thee the dear lost fields, look with thine eyes
On Erin's goodly men and gracious women.
Oh! yield me this: this my one joy fulfil.
I am not banished wholly, so I leave
My purpose planted in such breast as thine.

MOCHONNA.

How should I answer this? So dear a plea
Thrusts at me hard and through the harness-joints.
Yet no, and no, and no. 'Make passion wise?'
Passion is wise already, being passion:
She can because she would. 'Be free,' thou sayest.
Strongest is freest: strong am I, with thee.
'Live my own life?' Yea, will I. But that life
(Father, the Lord hath shown it me) is thine.
Ah! must I tell my story? Once a child
Was playing nigh a dim mid-forest cell.
There came a saint to pray. The child drew near
And watched him, awed. The up-flung head, the cowl
Stirred with the heart-throb, or a something (was it?)
Winnowing unviewed the air between them, held

His soul in a sweet terror, till the saint,
Arising, with his tranced eyes yet in heaven,
Fronted the boy, tarrying, too scared to flee.
Then the great light of those grey eyes came down
One moment, fell like an anointing flame,
So burningly, so tender; and one word
Fell with the light on the boy's heart, 'My son.'
The rest thou know'st.   I never told thee this.
Nor had I told at all, but now I see
That was God's moment when He sealed my soul;
God's moment, mighty as a thousand years.
All years of mine were in it, as the tree
Closed in the seed.   There did I choose, not here.
Nay, there was chosen.   All the after-hours
Danced to the rhythm of one enchanted name.
'Columba': all the wild wood throbbed with it.
'Columba': in the throngs of men I heard it.
If there were praising of high deeds, 'Columba'
I whispered to my heart.   All names were nought:
All pomps, all passions, all ambitions else
Were vacant shows, dumb echoes, meagre ghosts
Of one live worth that breathed and burned in thee.
I cannot image me the mortal doom
That holds not thee.   Therefore most sure am I
God wills it, for He set the yearning here:
God wills it,—for thou dar'st not question it.

See! I have moved thee, I have moved thee : yield.
Love is life's pilot ever ; let him rule :
Love, wise as Fate, Fate's kinder angel form ;
Heaven's cloudy pillar where it breaks a-flame ;
God's banner.   Let us follow it to the death.

COLUMBA.

Yea, to the red death or white age together,
Son, will we follow.   I clasp thee to my breast
Till the white age or the red death us part :
And with this kiss I seal thee Christ's and mine.
Oh! we the lonely virgin lives that miss
Earth's bridals and the father's fleshlier bond,
A hundredfold, yea in the life that is,
Receive we more.   God guard it ours.   Enough.
I cannot trust my words.   God keep it holy
In silence, this great bond that makes us one,
Till Christ declare it in His heaven of heavens.

Thou art the twelfth.   March with me to the war.

SCENE III.

On the Coracle. FECHNO *and* ERNAN *seated in the prow.*

FECHNO.

Didst mark that heron, Ernan, by the brink
At yonder point ?   We sent our ruffled wake
Up the tall shank to splash his skirts, and he
Stood with his musing chin pulled in, nor budged
An inch, nor stirred a feather.

ERNAN.

                  Yes, I saw.
Old solitary of the river wilds,
And day-long dreamer, half he seems to me
Monk of some sylvan Rule.   Why should he fear
His human brethren of the cowl ?

FECHNO.

                  Good wit.
But more I think, he knows the fowler's bonnet
And cowl apart.

ERNAN.

            Wise bird.   But I will hold
He is wiser yet.   He knows that out of Erin

Goes Erin's best : he comes to view the last
Of his great brother, and the kindest heart
That ever loved the woods and woodland folk.

FECHNO.

Yes, loves the woodland well ; and, were he not
Churchman, had loved it in another sort.
He has the forest eye, a hunter born
If ever any, as old Hubert vows.

ERNAN.

He has the woodcraft in a gentler kind :
He draws, not drives the creatures.   Baithen tells
How at his orisons the startled hare
Will turn and thread the thicket back, to peer
From the hazel root about his knees, as bold
As the quick bush-tailed climber in the bough.
'Tis Eden there for the wild folk and him.

.   .   .   .

COLUMBA (*in the stern*).

Come, brother Baithen, leave the oar awhile
And sit by me.   They need thee not : we make
Good speed, we exiles, all too good.   And thou
Dear son Mochonna, on the further side.

And give me each a hand, as marchers use
Who stem a stream together, when the glen
Is loud with wroth storm-water. Yea, for we
Have such a stream to cross, a river of death.

BAITHEN.

When our great Abbot needs to cross that stream,
There is no man of his would loose a hand.

COLUMBA.

Nay, simple-valorous one, I meant not so :
Though, truth, we soldiers make our count with death.
But, Baithen, there are other ways to die.
Death is that angel that unclothes the soul.
One while with sword or plague or age he rends
The garment of the flesh, to clothe anew
Or with pure, rosy vesture of the saint,
Or (God have mercy !) fire robe of the lost.
But with another hand, and yet austere,
He plucks the breathing man, spirit and frame
Together, from the warm enfolding life
Whereto he clung, one with it : plucks him forth
From home and friend and folk and land and kin,
From uses, helps, and proven instruments,
All purposes, all loves grown ripe with years,
And memory, nurse of hopes, and hopes that crown

Memory with starrier beauty—forth from these,
And casts him stark and sole, a naked mind,
Into the abyss to root him as he may.
Such image of a death 'tis ours to die.

MOCHONNA.

It is an image then, not death itself.
See our linked hands! we carry Erin with us
Fast in our mutual bosoms.

COLUMBA.

Ah! fair son,
Ever soft youth will lightlier part with life
Than our firm-rooted manhood. Thou perchance——.
Nay, but I thank thee for thy loyal word.
Nor speak I now of death as one who fears,
Or murmurs, any more. The pang is past.
Rather I taste a mystic joy to lie
One hour unclothed of temporal circumstance,
A naked soul by the All-Soul uplift,
Hid in the hollow of the Eternal's palm,
Mid-air between the worlds. Lo! now, our bark,
As if it bore a freight of spirits freed,
Leaving the long, long arms of the dear earth
Sternward, and winging for the twilight void,
Is climbing up and up the scaling seas,

Wave after wave, stair over stair, to win
Yon glimmering gate where ends the deep in heaven.
Ah! such a death the just made perfect die,
When all their works do follow them: not mine,
Not mine such death: my deeds are all to do,
My justness—God forgive me! But O friends,
Look back and tell me: is the headland hid?

BAITHEN.

Not hid, but faint already as a cloud
And blent with sky and water.

MOCHONNA.

See you there
That spark upon its edge! And look, it grows
Into a shoot of flame. What is it, Baithen?
Signal of war? How say you?

BAITHEN.

Ay, of war,
War surely: for to war we voyage. Nay;
A signal word of peace that spells, 'Farewell.'
'Tis Ronan and his fellows. With the dawn
(I knew of it) they went. They fire their pile
Still to be with us on the exile's foam
And linger out our Erin's last embrace.

COLUMBA.

What do they ?   Cruel love is here, to wake
An exile's pang.   I thought we had passed in peace
Like spirits of the blest; and now the earth
Checks, at the chain's length, backward her estray,
Nor hers again nor free.   'Twas ill bethought.
How couldst thou suffer it, Baithen ?

BAITHEN.

Pardon me.
I had not thought——.   They had a hunger for it,
To be the very last to speed the Abbot.
They warm their own chill bosoms at that blaze,
True hearts, not knowing.

COLUMBA.

Pardon *me*, my Baithen.
I am to blame that ever I blamed love,
Though the thorn pricked beneath the flower.   O friends
Who yet may stand on the dear soil, and wave
Your last of farewells, from the bitter sea
An exile's last of blessings light on you
With balm of all the sweetness he foregoes.

MOCHONNA (*after a pause*).

But Ronan, sire, thy Ronan—surely he
Should share our flight.   Was there no place for him?

COLUMBA.

My Ronan, say you?   Mine, and 'mine too much,'
They murmured.   Nay, no place for him with us.

MOCHONNA.

But wherefore?   It was spite and narrow heart
Girded at merry Ronan.   Care we for them?

COLUMBA.

No, not for them, son: not a jot for them.
For mine own sake I left him, and the work's.

MOCHONNA.

He would have cheered the work.   Stout heart was his
Under the lightsome mood and wandering eyes
And the frail limbs of him.   What song was that
Beside the camp-fire (but you heard it not)
That drooping night ere Connaught ranged with us?

Few, few, few !
From the brown moor's desolate ends,
From the cloud where the welkin blends,
  Plaineth the lone curlew.
    Few, few, few
  Feet to the gathering true,
  Feet on the heather of friends.

    Near, near, near,
With the grim day's labouring flight,
Cometh onward the southland might,
    Gathers the storm and the fear.
    Near, nearer, and near
  Dumb on the heather I hear
  Feet of the foes of the right.

And there he bent and listened long.   A tear
Rose, shining in the firelight: but it broke
Down-shaken, as the song-wind smote him again.

    Few our muster, and dark
  The camp of the hope forlorn.
Few—but amidst us are borne
    Prophet and hallowing ark.
      Few—but an answer, Hark !
  Faint through the severing dark:
  ' Few shall be many at morn.'

And with the dawn a shout ran in among us
From southward, and to arms we leapt, and met——
No foe, but Connaught's banners dancing in,
Ten thousand spears.   Nay, you remember that.

COLUMBA.

While I remember——.   But forbear.   Your Ronan
Would harp me back whither I would not.   Peace.
And look again, friends, if the land be hid.

MOCHONNA.

Not yet, nor will be.   Mark you how the wind,
That followed full, puffs on the leftward cheek.
Aedh changes course, steers for the northern star,
But eastward, wary of old Brecan's pool,
And keeps the land in touch.

COLUMBA.

                And all night long
Erin will overhang us, all night long
Reach yearning arms of dusky promontories
After her children.   We must yet endure,
Brothers, the long home-hunger.   But the wind
Of our great purpose, rising in its hour,
And bringing gales of strength, and blowing full
Our spirit's sail that flags in this sad air,

Will lift us onward.   O o'ershadowing God,
Who willest, ere we die, some deed be done,
Some deed by us unworthy, unto Thy
More glory and our less unworthiness,
Spread Thou Thy wing wide as the night is wide,
And in the utmost of the homeless sea
Let Thy hand find and lead : that neither blast,
Nor shoal, nor goring spear of secret rock,
Nor toppling wave, nor downward-eddying gulf,
Nor buffet of the fell sea-dragon's fin,
O'erwhelm us !   Some fair angel, on our prow
Alighting, with pure eyes o'erawe the deep
All night, until the whitening East unveil
The land Thou knowest whereon Thy name shall be.

ACT THIRD.

SCENE I.

Duni, the hill of Iona. COLUMBA *and* MOCHONNA *seated.*

MOCHONNA.

May I speak, father?

COLUMBA.

Surely.

MOCHONNA.

You have sat
A long hour silent, silent, gazing out
Southward, as if you saw Her.

COLUMBA.

Ay, too clear.

MOCHONNA.

And then you turned; 'twas when beyond the sound
One hailed our ferry: though you looked not thither,
But swept the little plain, rock, heather, tilth,
And pasture, with a lone and weary glance,
As when one seeks and misses.

COLUMBA.

Like enow.

Something I missed.

MOCHONNA.

Your thought is lightly read,
Father: the day comes round, as by the year.
I said, 'The old wound galls him with the day.'

COLUMBA.

No, the old wound galls not.

MOCHONNA.

Why then, what new?

COLUMBA.

Nay, nor a new.

MOCHONNA.

Yet you are sad, more sad
Than e'er I knew you in this manner.   I fear
To ask your trouble, father: but I ask.

COLUMBA.

I thought on grey Molasius, and the Isle.   .   .   .

[*Pauses.*

MOCHONNA.

Good cause have you to think of him.   I too.

COLUMBA.

The grey, lone saint.   The little sea-bound isle.   .   .   .

MOCHONNA.

You are not sad for him.   He loves it well.

COLUMBA (*impetuously*).

But I, I cannot love it.   O my son,
Chilling it came upon me—' here is mine;
My isle, the prison of my penance; here
Shall I waste out my summers.'

MOCHONNA.

Waste them ?   How ?

What likeness holds ?   We came to war, not dream.
Not island hermit, island soldier thou.

COLUMBA.

And there are soldiers die without the deed.

MOCHONNA.

Not thou.

COLUMBA.

And why not I ?

MOCHONNA.

Nay, wherefore fear it ?
Our deed has opened fairly : we have sped.
There lies our camp of wattles, in the fence
Of girdling sea.   To-morrow o'er the sound
(Serve wind) we row the timbers home, and build
Our shrine, the fortress whence Columba moves
To conquer Alba.

COLUMBA.

If it be to conquer.

MOCHONNA.

You doubt it ? you ?

COLUMBA.

No sin to doubt, if faith
Outran her warrant.   Son, my cloud has fallen.
We trusted—did we well to trust ?   The deed,
So goodly, seemed the warrant for itself.
There went a fire to lead me : eagle wings
Upbare me coming : they have left me thus,
Lightless, and wingless, and the pathway lost.
Nay, sadden not, Mochonna, till you hear.
I trust the good hand of my God ; I trust.
But some there are He bears to golden dooms,
Full-measured with the signs that led them.   Some
He lifts awhile, glorying, on eagle wings,
To drop on deserts, on an aching doom
Of silence, deedless ends, a nameless grave.
My heart misgives me, such an end is mine.
I hear the men who speak, remembering me,
' His star rode high, Columba : but he went
Somewhere to the wild folk, and there an end.'
God's will !   But hard, Mochonna, hard to bear.

MOCHONNA.

Thy cloud, not ours, has fallen.   Us who sit
But in the skirts, it blinds not, though it chill.
Thy brethren see not with thy sight, those eyes

That see the stars where we but sunlight.   No.
Nor with thy darkness are we dark.   The sun
Yet rides the sky for us, when veiled for thee.
Use our sight then, till the seer's own return.

COLUMBA.

Why, be it so.   Thy vision then, my son.

MOCHONNA.

I see—but how to tell thee ?—yet—why there
(Look, father, look) the word is spoken for me.
I see grim Alba's mountains, fold on fold ;
Storm in their glens.   But toward them from the isle,
Sails such a sunbeam o'er the sound, and breaks
Wavelike upon the kindled coast, and scales
To fire the cloud-bow on their fuming tops.
My word is spoken there.   For O what cloud,
Blacker than storm, over those sullen hills,
What darkness of what cruel homes of men,
Waits for our Island's Light !   And must it wait,
Columba on the threshold ?   This to do:
And thou to do it: and the thing undone !
Or will the Almighty hide the polished shaft
Long in His hollow palm, to break it then,
Then, when the battle joins ?   If this can be
What worth is faith ?

　　　　　　　Ah! I am rash, as ever:
For so your eyes reprove me.

COLUMBA.

　　　　　　　　　Nay, not rash.
'Tis a boy's faith, but blessed, and strong to win.
Hold it.　But know, there is a riper faith
And sadder, humbling all the soul in dust,
That whispers, 'Does God need Columba so?
Has not the potter power upon the clay
To make, or break, to cast upon the heap
The vessel freshest from the wheel and best?'
Ah! yes: and half the mighty world is dark;
Yet how God waits to say, 'Let there be light.'
Hold, boy, thy faith.　It cannot answer mine.

MOCHONNA.

You are hard to answer, father.　Yet the mood
Will change.　But let me leave you for a while,
To learn what means yon stir about our boat
New touched, a stranger on her, and return.

COLUMBA (*alone*).

'The little plain,' he said, 'the little plain.'
How little all things look this barren morn!
All shrinks with the shrunk spirit.　But afar

What world of iron hills and heathen glens,
Vastness that breaks the hope, a wilderness
To swallow up men's lives, and nothing done.
What ! is my heart turned coward now, and faints
At the edge of war ?   I am not used to faint
At battle.   Nay, not fear is this : the truth
Strikes home, it is the penance of my sin.
' The toil, son, be thy penance,' said the seer.
Not so.   I came to suffer and to work :
I bide to suffer and waste—the hermit's end
Not soldier's mine, nor shepherd's.   God's high will.
God's ?   Is it His ?   Not as He willed it, then,
But as I warped it sinning.   There's the sting
That makes obedience bitter, woe's my heart !
I dreamed I paid the utmost toll of sin
Dying the death of exile.   Dreamed.   For here
The imperious shadow fronts me in the path,
Reaching a hand to take the new life too.
It met me that first hour I crossed the isle.
For, resting in a seaward grassy lawn
Hung with low cliffs, I looked, and on the walls
What hand had writ my shame ?   From cleft and scar,
Dyeing with flecks the grey cliff face, methought,
Sweated red oozings as of blood.   I quailed
At the omen.   Then I mocked it.   ' Nature's freak ;
Time's rust upon them.'   Yet my guilty veins

H

Curdled, as if the wounds of all my slain
Welled up to witness that the slayer was nigh.
Horrible! and I held me purged! Alas!
To purge the soul makes not to free the life.
This mortal bears its trespass yet. My years,
Drawn by their secret chain for ever down,
Will fail their golden mark, and, crownless, end
In some bleak grave beside the stranger sea.

    [*Enter* MOCHONNA, *with a* DALRIAD *of the mainland.*

MOCHONNA.

Sire, here is one will speak but with yourself.

COLUMBA.

What would you, friend?

DALRIAD.

               A shelter, holy sire,
To save a hunted life new plucked from death.

COLUMBA.

What death? what hunters?

DALRIAD.

                  Heathen of the north.
A Dalriad, sire, am I, of Erin's kin
In Britain. Five nights since, the raiding Pict

Broke on and fired our steading, haled us thence,
Brother with me, and sister : him my eyes
(And that accurst fire burns yet in my blood)
Saw on their demon-altar bound and burned.
God heat sevenfold the furnace of their hell,
So grant He first my will upon them.   Her——
Father, I know not if she died, or lives
A death more miserable, the heathen's thrall.
For me—by chance unhoped, that drunken night
Which revelled out the horror, I slipped my cord,
'Scaped, the chase hot upon my heels, and turned
Because I would not draw the Pictish sword
Down on my tribesmen, shoreward : there, good hap,
Found friends and boat and quiet seas, and came,
Great father, to entreat for sanctuary.

                                  [A pause.

Shall I not have it ?—of thy faith, thy blood.

                                  [A pause.

(*To* MOCH.) Young sir, he speaks not. Do I plead in vain?

MOCHONNA.

Fear not: some thought o'ercomes him.   'Tis his mood.

COLUMBA (*to himself*).

Upon the demon-altar !   Christ !   And Thou
Wast offered once.

DALRIAD.

Yea, on their altar, sire—
My brother.   Christ's curse burn them, flesh and soul!

COLUMBA (*looking up*).

Man!   What hath Christ with curses?

DALRIAD.

O the fire,
And the eyes that stared from out it!   I but live
To whet the sword that slakes it in their blood.

COLUMBA (*to himself*).

How long, how long?

DALRIAD.

Ay, every hour is long
That lets me.   But I wait, wait, wait.   It comes.
Till then but give me shelter.

COLUMBA.

Yes, it comes.
Else wherefore was I born?   It comes indeed.

DALRIAD.

Yea, father: so we wait.

COLUMBA.

Wait ?   Not an hour.
Wait ?   God in heaven ! and such deeds done on earth !
Wait ?   I go forth to-morrow.

DALRIAD.

Ah ! no, no.
To-morrow cannot be.   You know them not,
How many, and what fighters, of what wile.
And fast they hold together, Pict by Pict,
To where Brude sits far on the eastern sea.
No.   Bide awhile, till they forget us.   Then
We creep one moonless midnight round their huts,
Seven spears at every door ; and shout and stroke
Shall be as thunder and bolt when both are one,
And not a life break through our hedge of thorns
To tell whose hand fell on them.

MOCHONNA.

He hears you not :
He would not brook your counsel, if he heard.

DALRIAD.

Nay, then, what better ?   Men must bide the hour.

COLUMBA (*looking up*).

The hour, the hour! It is thy trumpet, God.
I am ready, I am ready.

DALRIAD.

Sire, be ruled.

COLUMBA.

Ah! friend, I had forgotten you. Forgive—
And yet—what chieftain, said you, in the east?

DALRIAD.

Brude. He that holds Craig Phadrick: but his word
Sways every chief of Picts between the seas.

COLUMBA.

Then we go thither.

DALRIAD.

God forbid it thee.
Madness. You go but to their demon-fires.

COLUMBA (*rising*).

Man, there is fire within me that will blanch
Whiter than any ash their fires of bale.
We shall avenge him well—your brother—well;
Yea, on the demons. God, the trumpet is it.

And I to doubt if there were deeds for me!

O light of all the dark of all the world,

O holy flame of the blest sacrifice,

O fire of Love, dying that these might live,

Shine in me living, dying: shine through me

On these red slayers, brothers of my guilt,

Guiltless, who know not what they do. Awake,

Arm of the Lord; I follow: the deed shall be.

(*To the* DALRIAD.) But come, sir, I have much to learn
    of you.

DALRIAD.

(*To* MOCH.) What like of man is this? He mazes me.

                                     [*Goes.*

MOCHONNA (alone).

He mazes *me.* Heaven! how the great grey eyes

Widened, as if the Light he called upon

Sphered itself there! I saw it once, but once,

This glory. 'Twas that hour I passed unknown

Hard by him into battle. I peered and saw.

Wonderful! all the tumult of my flesh

And terror died in a great quiet, as if

God's finger touched the flesh and freed the soul.

I could fear nothing after. And this look

Was like, yet other. What a man is here!

SCENE II.

The tent of the missionaries near Craig Phadrick, the
fortress of Brude, King of the Picts.

BAITHEN *enters.*

BAITHEN.

How do you now, Mochonna?

MOCHONNA.

　　　　　　　　　　　Well at ease.
The fever shakes me not: my mind is grown
So clear and lightsome, that it augurs me
Some issue great and glad is hard at hand.

BAITHEN.

'Tis like, Mochonna.　Can you see yon hill,
Not far, but dim in starlight, level-ridged?

MOCHONNA.

Surely.　What of it?

BAITHEN.

　　　　　　　　　'Tis the seat of Brude.

MOCHONNA.

That is the gate, then, where we knock to-morrow.

BAITHEN.

To-morrow.   *There* is issue great enough.

MOCHONNA.

And glad, my brother, glad,—howe'er it fall.

BAITHEN.

Yea.   But the waiting.   With what iron tread
March on the ponderous hours, with what bleak light
The steel-hard stars look down.   'Tis thus, methinks,
A soldier feels before the fighting morn.

MOCHONNA.

You to have said it, Baithen!   So he feels.
I know it, though it is my shame to know.
Ah! yes: the watchful stars that note and hide
The couching soldier's secret: the live hush
Of beating hearts: and yon dim lift of hill
That we must carry with the dawn—how like
That other night (good omen!) ere we won;
As we shall win to-morrow.   We?   Alas!

I

I that fought with him the unhallowed fight,
Fight not the holy; this marsh fever's clutch
So lets me from the ranks.

BAITHEN.

                    Nay, brother, cheer.
When we have won, there will be work enough
To share: or, if——

MOCHONNA.

                    Why fear to end it? 'If
We fail, then death to share.' Ah! Baithen, death
Is hard, for all the glory, save with him.
Love casteth fear out; and I too could die
Under his eyes. Without him . . .

BAITHEN.

                    Hist! Mochonna.
One passes yonder by the trees. Aedh is it
Upon his watch?

MOCHONNA.

                    No watcher's footstep that.
And see, between the trunks he pauses, clear
On open sky, turned to the Pictish hill.
Ah! now you know him.

BAITHEN.

        Yes.   The lifted hands.
He sends his prayer before him up the hill.
Courage! That prayer will leap the rampart, steal
Through those strong guards, and, at the prince's side,
Murmuring in pagan ears they know not whence
A word they hearken not yet heed, unstring
The arm of hasty violence, ere it lift
Hand on the Lord's Anointed. Brother, cheer;
Good cheer: we are not set for death to-morrow

SCENE III.

The tent.

MOCHONNA (*alone*).

Steps on the turf! It is the news. O Christ!
                         [BAITHEN *enters.*
Speak it not. Let me read it . . . Ah! 'tis well.
Yet you look awed too. Speak: I bear it now.

BAITHEN.

O brother, be there wonders yet on earth?
We went, the Abbot, Ernan, and myself,

And the boy thrall who taught their speech, and Ronan,
Ay, Ronan, with that harp which grows to him
Like a fifth limb (the elf), to where the hill
Grows bare below the fortress. There he stayed,
And casting a high look and tender, 'Friends,
Tarry,' he said, 'I go the rest alone.'
How we cried out against it, image you.
'Nay, lest we quench,' he said, 'the lamps of all
Together': then to me, 'Good Baithen, stay:
For who shall guide the brethren, if I fall?'
So went he forth alone. But Ronan, he,
(What dares not Ronan?) dancing after him,
Looked quaintly up, and whispered him. The face
Frowned; but a smile broke through. 'Ay, Ronan, ay.
We ever fight together.' So they came
Gateward. We heard the challenge, 'Open, ho!
An envoy waits.' A dozen wolfish heads
Stared o'er the rampart, silent: then a laugh
Bellowed, of barbarous throats. Half-oped the door.
One parleyed through it, and Columba cried,
'Tell him, the envoy of my king and his.'
Bellowed a noisier laughter; clashed the door.
Then,—blame my eyes for folly—but I saw
A hand that waved, signing the cross, and wide,
As if God's breath had blown it from its bar,
Swung the great door inward. I saw no more:

But, torn between obedience and my love,
Broke loose, and bounded after up the slope ;
There found a tumult dying, grounded spears,
Low murmurs, wondering eyes, but nowhere him.
Then through the throng slipt Ronan, pale, uplit
With such a pure and steady light as never
Shone, brother, in those dancing eyes, and said
'Baithen, we win, we win.   Go tell the rest,
(He bade me say it) Christ hath kept His own.'
I know not why I did not question more.
I was amazed, abashed : I turned, I came,
And told—this broken story.

MOCHONNA.

                         'Tis enough.
Christ keeps His own : he lives.   O glad am I,
How glad, you stayed no moment more.   He lives.
Dear Baithen, when you went, I lay and stared
Before me, mindless, strengthless, could not make
One little prayer to follow you : my life
Was gone the while with him, my clay was here.
Then came, I think, the fever-folly, I saw
Columba by me, in his hand a palm.
He spoke not, but with eyes I could not read
Searched mine.   I reached to touch him : 'twas a babe
Grasping at stars, he was so far away.

I murmured, 'Saint of the red martyrdom
In glory:' but it wrung me like a pang,
And woke me weeping, weeping. Then your step,
Your eyes; and I thanked heaven my dream was vain.

BAITHEN.

My thanks with yours. I shame to grudge the palm:
But ere we feast with saints, I pray to drink
This earthlier-holy wine of brotherhood
Full measure in his love and yours, Mochonna.
But tell me of yourself. Your eyes are bright
And not with fever; and there's blood again
Filling your lips.

MOCHONNA.

   Your news is cordial.
Some Pict shall be my convert yet. But, hark
'Tis Ronan, or I know not Ronan's tread.

RONAN (*entering*).

I kiss your hand, loved sir: grow well and live,
For there are flocks in Britain for your hand.

MOCHONNA.

Kind Ronan, I believe it. But thy lord——

RONAN.

Has conquered.   Surely Baithen told you all.

BAITHEN.

I told but what I heard, that all was well:
And what I saw, the wonder at the gates.

RONAN.

The wonder at the gates?

BAITHEN.

                    Yea, when he signed
The cross, and they flew wide before him.

RONAN.

                                        Ay?
And did he so?   Marry, he set his hand—
God wot, he has the thews of Finn—I know
The gates flew wide enough, and we were in;
And from the dust the tumbled doorkeeper
Stared up, too mazed to hinder.   But there rose
A scurry and a shout: a score of spears
Hung at our eyes.   Silent he looked them o'er,
And seemed to grow and grow.   For me, I felt
Nor fear nor daring; in a stupid muse

I watched my fate as 'twere some other man's.
And yet those murdering hands fell not: I think
His eyes unsinewed them: across my brain
Half a prayer flickered; then a great voice raug
'Let be:' and in his doors a warrior rose
Red-bearded, huge, unarmed, with eyes of scorn.
Then all gave back, and those two goodly men
(I know not which was mightier, monk or king)
Looked each in other's eyes, and no man spake.
Sudden Columba stirred: as prince to prince
He stept with offered hand: the other hung
A moment with pressed lip and rolling eyes;
Then heaved the russet beard, the deep eye flashed
From menace into welcome, King's hand met
Abbot's, and all my stayed veins leapt again:
For now is Britain ours.

BAITHEN.

So fast, my Ronan?

RONAN.

Where jumps the big bell-wether jump the flock.
No chief of them dares touch the guest of Brude.

BAITHEN.

Well, well: you have more to tell us.

RONAN.

Nay, not I.
When I came back from you, the doors were shut
On king and abbot.   Down I sat to wait.
The big guards came and stared at me, like dogs
That watch some little, unknown, woodland thing
And fear to try it.   Long they stared : at last
Into my finger-tips the frolic ran,
Round came my harp, I taught them how we won
Culdrevny fight.   O to have laughed my laugh
(I dared not) when those beamy shanks began
To feel the lusty rhythm and swing the knee.
A minute more, I had had my troop of bears
A-dancing : but hark ! hush ! the music broke ;
A door creaked ; 'twas Columba facing me,
Shaking his brows, but O I caught the smile
Flashed in an eyelid's flicker.   ' Bard,' he said,
' Go take your music homewards : tell them I
Am with them ere an hour.'   So home I came.
The tale is his.

BAITHEN.

Till then, Mochonna, rest.
Come, bard, without, for you must tease your strings
To yield us the new war-song.   Rest you well.

K

MOCHONNA (*alone*).

Peace, peace, and peace! O ease of aching nerve
After the daring and the dread. I think
To die can be no other, when the soul,
A passage-bird that beats a fainting wing
Over cold seas, and holds the air with pain,
Sudden will breast the upbearing wind of heaven,
And stir no plume, but float and float and fall
Into the Eternal's bosom.

[*Sleeps.*

SCENE IV.

The same. COLUMBA *enters.*

MOCHONNA (*waking*).

Thou? or thy shade again?

COLUMBA.

Nay, by this hand
Laid on thy brows, no shadow. Live thou too,
For He has willed His glory by our life.

MOCHONNA.

Yea, thou.   This time I touch thee.   O beloved
A hundredfold from the awful pass of death.
I have no care to question.   Thou art here,
Thy hand on me, thine eyes.   I would no more.

COLUMBA.

No care to question?   Nay, nor I to tell,
For gladness at thy health.   Son, from this bed
Such trouble went with us, our peril seemed
Phantom-like by the fears we left.   And now
The great joy tastes not for my joy in thee.

MOCHONNA.

The joys are one.   We live to work the work.

COLUMBA.

As God has willed us work it.   How my veins
Beat with the wonder, as that warrior's mind
Lay grasped in mine, to handle how I would,
As when a man's hand folds about a child's:
Greatest in Britain, in God's kingdom least.
Greatest?   He is that no longer: One there is
Greater than Brude in Britain, One there is
Will rule the ruler. . . Out on't!   O son, son!

Thy asking look.   My angel's chiding eyes
Had never pierced me deeper.

MOCHONNA.

What is this?

I read you not.

COLUMBA.

No, but your innocent eyes,
That cannot read me, make me read myself:
So clear a soul looks through them: I the while
Hide such a coiling secret in my own.

MOCHONNA.

Forbear.   You shame me.

COLUMBA.

And 'tis you, my son,
Must charm that serpent forth.

MOCHONNA.

Ah! could I that!
Sire, what is this new trouble?

COLUMBA.

Alas! not new.
The fiend that lost me Erin, haunts me here.

MOCHONNA.

The fiend of violence, mean you ?   Dead he lies,
Dead with the thrice-dead past.

COLUMBA.

                      Yea, lies he so ?
Who ever buried yet his past ?   But this
Is deadlier than that brawling fiend of feud,
Being his subtler master.   'Tis the pride
Of the heart that cannot rest unless it rule.

MOCHONNA.

God made the strong for rule.   What sin is here ?

COLUMBA.

O virgin spirit, and stainless but for me,
Didst ever thou (but no, I think it not)
Pursue some holy vision of a deed,
Grasp it : and lo ! its fashion changed, and there. .
What in your arms lay but your olden sin,
Smiling its cursèd smile, victor again ?
Son, when I climbed yon hill, my heart was peace,
Pure, all-subduing, all-upholding peace.
So simple was it : I should die, or live.
And God, not I, must choose it now : my will

Moved on in His, nor knew itself apart
More than the lifted billow knows itself
From the deep tide that swings it toward the shore.
So.   But I did not die.   We sat, we talked,
The chief of Britain and the chief of Hy,
He of the little isle the greater.   Then
Even as I preached the Christ, the selfless king,
Began a Christless king, the kingly self
That broke my peace and broke my Erin's peace,
To stir and swell and glory in my veins.
' Move this, move Britain,' came the thought : again .
' What, have I lost the sway to find the sway ? '
And still the proud dream shaped itself, and still
I preached the Christ : but with the tale of grace
The graceless burden of a heathen hope
Blent in my ears who told it, as the harp
Of Ronan unawares at distance blends
Wild music with our psalm.   I sinned the sin
(Nor knew it) that hath lost Columba once,
And yet may lose him.   But I know it now,
Since thy pure eyes fell on it.   Son, my son,
I was thy soul's-friend ever, be thou mine,
Who have no elder : be thou mine, and hold
Thy selfless nature's faithful crystal up
To glass and give to view the spirit of ill
That whispers at thy father's ear.

Alas !
What do I, thus to strain thy weakness ?   Rest ;
Forget it.   Nay, or I will sit with thee,
Holding thy hand in mine a little while,
And tell the long day's wonders, point by point,
Gently and low, till the sleep falls again.

ACT FOURTH.

SCENE I.

The landing-place at Derry. A.D. 575. *Before the Synod of Drumceit.* ERNAN *and a* RETAINER *of* FERGUS.

RETAINER.

Ernan! Our twelve-year parted Ernan back!
Why, then I'll yet believe it.

ERNAN.

What is this,
Old friend, I am such warrant for?

RETAINER.

They say,
Columba comes to Erin again, Columba!

ERNAN.

Yea, to Drumceit, to parley with the kings.

RETAINER.

Yea, but the vow ! I marvelled at the news.
How said yon hermit of the western rock ?
'Never again to Erin, never again.'

ERNAN.

Why then you know not how Molasius sent
(Last breath the grey seer cast on mortal air),
'Go tell Columba, "not the Lord but I."
Thou hast the spirit of Christ. I pass. Be thou
Thy doomster for the rest.'

RETAINER.

              The doom is good
That speeds him home to Erin. Will he now
Teach our hot Aedh to loose the Dalriad's fee
And homage of our Erin over-seas ?

ERNAN.

Sooth, the task craves a master. O but he,
Mighty for wars, is mightier yet for peace.
I had not dreamed it of him ; no, not I.

RETAINER.

He stilled old riotous Brecan, so they tell,
That roared to gulf him. May he swim as sure

L

The land swirl of our Council! But our Aedh,
Who loves his glorious clansman of the cowl,
Less loves the clansman's heart should spend itself
On Aidan's fledgeling greatness.

ERNAN.

　　　　　　　　'Tis to fear.
But I do think more nigh the Abbot's heart
Lies the Bards' danger. Ill the quarry fares
When folk and king are hounds and huntsman.

RETAINER.

　　　　　　　　　　　　　　　　Ay,
The Bards, our song-birds which we petted till
They peck the petting hand in wantonness,
And filch the dainties from the board. And yet
Pity to drive or dumb our songsters. Well,
'Tis your Lord's proper quarrel: Prince of Bards
Should be Bards' Champion. Turn it how it may,
He is full welcome home, and welcomer
The more he make it home.

ERNAN.

　　　　　　　　How mean you, friend?

RETAINER.

O there be those will tell him that. Our House

Miss him too long; and, since the vow is out,
Perchance his isle will spare him.

ERNAN.

Sir, my task
(Forgive me) somewhat calls on haste. I think
I may not parley longer. With your leave
I take my farewell of you.

[*Goes.*

RETAINER.

Whew! my friend
Flushed angerly. Ill promise, if like man
Like master. He was ever cloister-bird,
Ernan, and grudged Columba to his kin.

SCENE II.

Drumceit. FERGUS *and* COLUMBA.

FERGUS.

And must you part to-morrow?

COLUMBA.

Yes, to-morrow,
While the seas sleep.

FERGUS.

Then will you part too soon.

COLUMBA.

Why should I tarry, friend ?   Our work is done.
At home they need me.

FERGUS.

Ay, they need you sore
. . . At home.   And therefore would I bid you stay.

COLUMBA.

A riddle, Fergus.

FERGUS.

One that you can read.

COLUMBA.

And lightly : those truth-speaking eyes of yours
Have read it for me.   Friend, it cannot be.

FERGUS.

Why 'cannot'?   O great cousin, hear me once.
I have watched you at the Council, seen you sway
Our headlong lords, as they were brawling boys

Awed by a man. I said, ' My cousin's fire
Burns steadier, but it burns as strong, as when
We broke stout Diarmid,' you and I together,
My sword, your counsel. Ha ! have you forgot ?

COLUMBA.

No ; else would Fergus plead with better hope.

FERGUS.

O but remember, cousin ; when the rest
Had so much warcraft as a bull, to set
Head down and counter them, brute horn to horn,
Ha ! ha ! 'twas you and I, old comrade, met
Beside the oak in the low moon, and traced
Our battle in the dust, and how my men
Should creep and creep round Diarmid's sleepy flank
To weave the raft of shields, and flat-long thread
His fencing quagmire, light as river-rats
Buoyed on a float of lily leaves. I caught
Your hand, and called you ' brother-soldier'; you
—You started like a dreamer, were not pleased.
O but that cowl of yours hid thrice the wit
For battle of our helmets.

COLUMBA.

Fergus, cease.

You know not how you plead against your plea.
I will not sin it twice.

FERGUS.

Nor I will tempt.
Your pardon for remembering.　But, Columba,
It is not now as then.　That too I saw
In council, when your Aidan's patience broke
In taunts : Aedh started, flaming, and went dumb ;
And all we hushed, waiting the bolt : but you
(What is that mastery that abashes us,
Strange kinsman, in your voice ?) you only said
—But 'twas as if one spoke it from the air—
' Brothers, we are one Erin, there as here.
Peace.'　And a peace there was.　O stay with us.
You came in Britain's aid, abide in ours,
The healer of our feuds.

COLUMBA.

The healer ?　I ?
Fate turns her wheel apace then.　Nay, my friend.
This might have been.　I am all Britain's now.

FERGUS.

All Britain's ?　All the blood of all your veins
Cries out on you for treason.　Erin's once

Is Erin's ever.   But I know for all
The twelve sad exile summers, hers are you.
For this is home, Columba : never Gael
Forgot the nursing-mother.   Said I 'mother'?
Why she, the very mother of your blood,
Eithnè, who saw your glories in the dream,
Pleads with me from the silent land of souls.
Her people are thy people, and they crave,
Because the times go ill, a leader.   Who
Should stead the men of Leinster as thyself,
Leinster's great son ?   You shake the head.   You think
I talk of hostings, plottings.   Cousin, no.
In this loud world of arms there moves a power
(We swordsmen know it) that can clear a path
More surely than the sword-sway, takes the heart
Captive behind the levelled steel, and wins
Unwounding and not wounded.   God who makes
Knows of what stuff 'tis made : I know it thine.
Lo ! you would rob the household of your gift,
To squander it on strangers, cast your pearls—
Nay, then, I'll speak no scorn of your wild men :
They love you : sooth ! the fault were else their own—
But, kinsman, kinsman, blood is blood.   You slight
(I brave you saying it), but indeed, you slight
High nature's holy bond that makes men one,
Her sacrament of kinship.   And for what ?

For Alba of the Ravens, homeless Alba,
Rocks of the sea-mew, moors of kite and crow,
For heathendom's raw hearth and witless heart !
O but it grieves my soul our man of men,
Our own heaven-dowered Columba, Erin's star,
Whose beam God kindled for her storied field,
Should fail his mark, misprize his birthright, waste
A royal spirit's wealth unthanked, and starve
A golden doom on naked isles of storm.

COLUMBA.

Moved are you, Fergus.   You were little used
To flow in words.   These would have moved myself
If I might hearken words of men.   But cease.
I may not yield; and it is pain to hear.

FERGUS.

But would my counsel pain you, were it nought ?
Farewell—until to-morrow.

[*Exit.*

COLUMBA.

                         ' Till to-morrow.'
Will it be then ' farewell ' ?   His words are wind
That blows a rolling sea, swayed from beneath
Already : they but break it into voice.
Come back to Erin, at the council board

It sounded: 'back to Erin,' in the choirs
Of chanting Derry.   Ancient longings, thinned
By distance, like the sorcerer's viewless line
Which hales his captive, clench upon me here
Cords as of steel.   Why came I back, to set
Foot in an open snare?   Nay, 'twas not I
Came, but God brought me.   Other was there none
Could loose these knots save with the sword.   I came
By the priest's bond, peacemaker.   Is it God
Tempts my obedience but to temper it?
Why, let Him take this sword of His, my soul,
And in the fieriest furnace of desire
Torture white-hot, to plunge the shuddering grain
In the stark ice-bath of what loneliest doom
He chooses for me.   I would joy in it:
If I but knew, if I but knew.   For oh!
What if He tempts me not, but rather calls
His servant to new venture?   That might be.
How said the island saint of silence?   'Trust
Man's nature, 'tis God's oracle.'   He said it.
Shall I not trust this prophet in my breast,
This craving heart which craves because it can,
And bid it set my task?   What work is here
For me!   My very work; my fingers fret
To have the handling of it.   Here to reign
Their unnamed, viewless, spiritual king,

M

Centring in one deft hand a hundred clues,
Seeing a goal they see not, steering to it
These blind and restive champions, unaware.
O I could salve these rancours, awe to peace
Neil of the North, Neil of the South, could stay
The blood-rain of our fields, let princes die
On the down pillow, shriven.　Ha! why, so.
Thus I unsin my sin, pay back to Erin
For each life slain a thousand!　Can there be
A fate so apt, and God not mean it?

　　　　　　　　　　　　　　　　　　Ah!

Too confident Columba, is the fate
So apt then, or so sure?　Is't you would rule
The princes, or the princes you?　I fear
Earth's children on the vantage-field of earth
Are stronger than the saints.　The wings that range
High heaven, but stoop to rescue, dare not perch,
Lest they be limed.　Why, my own Fergus, best
And sanest of the stormy brotherhood,
Seeks to the monk but for a holier charm
To smooth the worldly way.　A peril here
To count with!　On my narrow sea-lapped rock,
That least of kingdoms, where my hold of earth
Is dwindled to a pin-point, earth I touch
Light as a footless ghost nor mingle with it.
But on the broad and unfenced, equal plain,

In the hot breath and jostle of the herd,
Will the soul guard her clearness? Peril here.

Well, there is peril then. God made the saints
For peril. Would He leave His world of men
Unpiloted, for fear the pilot drown,
Sunk with the ship? And I was framed for men,
To mingle with, subdue them. Not for me
The mute home of unneighboured solitude
Our Cormac hungers for and hunts in vain
All the seas over. And I think that God
Hath for such rare ordeal annealed me well
By trespass and the fruit of trespass, then
By pilgrim sojourn and the severing years
Through which I died to passion. Danger, yes.
Danger there is. And I am armoured for it.

But then my Britain. They will cry on me,
'We are thy children, thou hast travailed with us
Till we should live in Christ. Leave us not thou;
We claim a parent's pledge. Who made the life
Must rear it.' Children, I shall answer you,
'Ye are strong sons in faith, no babes, to need
Babes' milk and eyes of watching. Kenneth bides
And Cormac, men that have one tongue with you,
And my strong Baithen in his prime of years,

Steward of all our memories, all our hopes,
And stronger if I leave his side unfenced;
And with them—but I know not—nay, not he. . . .
What would ye, sons?   I am God's shepherd, I;
Shepherd not master of the sheep, to lead
What flock He bids me in what fields He wills,
So I be sure He wills it.'

                        Ah! 'be sure.'
But there's the pain: for who can surely know?
How easy now to end it thus, 'O soul,
Choose safely; take the hard, forsake the sweet.
Is Erin dear?   Then cast this love away,
A costly-fragrant balm of sacrifice
Outpoured for Who is dearer.'   Yes, 'tis easy.
Is it so safe?   Or can one safely choose
Who only chooses safety?   God Who bids
We add to virtue, knowledge, bids me here
With all the pith and sinew of my mind
Discern the truth and follow it, dread or dear.
But ah! till I discern, the travail of it!

Father, who watchest in Thy silent heaven,
Knowing the right, bidding me know it, yet
Unconquerably silent, till I choose,
Oh! in the dizzying, weary to and fro,
And counter-winds of question, in the blank

And shoreless void of doubt, where steers a soul,
Let me not err, Father of souls, not err.
Thou wilt not speak.   Yea, Lord, but let the hand
Bar the false path in silence.   [*A pause.*

       Doubters once,
When thought's slow balance dallied long, would weight
The tedious scale with any grain of sand,
Cry of an owl, a crow's flight, idle sounds
Caught from the babbling market.   Were they fools
To judge the gods were kind and would not leave
Man's path without a signal ?

        Music there !
A random chord, a bard that passes.

        [RONAN *enters.*
      You !
I scarce have seen you since the council made
The peace between your Order and the folk.

RONAN.

Pardon it, master.   Ah ! how worn a look !
And that is strange in you.   Our champion
Has spent some strength to save us.

COLUMBA.

       Nay, not so.
Am I so worn ?   Not in your quarrel then,

Dear minstrel.   But the medicine is yours.
Come, I have saved your harps, and earned the song.

RONAN.

And have it, master, all your own : the woods
Alone have heard it yet.   But what a song !
A brief bird-flight, two beats of music's wing ;
No more.   Yet flights of birds, you told me once,
Were signs of things to be for ancient men.
(*Sings.*)
    Waters of doom that drowned an earth,
        A sea with never a shore.
    And what is it wings to the wandering hearth
        That travels the void sea-floor ?
            Lost in the surf and the heave,
            Seen on the rose-red of eve,
    Clear in the skies ere it stoop to the haven,—
    Ah ! 'tis no wing of our rover the Raven ;
            Soft to her harbour of love
            Steadies and settles the dove.

    A land of brothers, a land of war :
        A flock that the grim wolf grips.
    And who is the white-clad helper afar,
        Lo ! and with peace in the lips ?

Lost for a day and a day,
Saved to fair Erin for aye,
Hither from Alba, grey roost of the raven,
Homeward there steers o'er the desert foam-paven,
Ah! unforgettingly well
Homeward, our Dove of the Cell.

I have not pleased you. Is my song too bold?
Sire, I am but a mocking-bird who hears
What all men say, and sings it to your face.

COLUMBA.

I was misdoubting, Ronan, of your lore.
The parable runs lame. Your homeward dove
Went outward yet again, and came no more.

RONAN.

Then hear another parable of the birds:
Yea, of an island-sojourner, who winged
Again to Erin and back no more to Hy.
(*Sings.*)
'Stranger Grey-wing, whence and whither
From the sea-cloud drift you hither
Sorely spent;

Glazing eye and pinion dragging,
Like a shipman's sail down-sagging
    Tempest-rent?
    Know, you come to Alba's coast,
    Heron, and a tender host.'

'Spent am I and nigh to perish.
Take me, tender host, and cherish
    Safe; and then
Let me rise and back to yonder
Happy West, that bare me, wander
    Home again.
    Take me, kindred hands of Hy:
    Ye are Erin's, Erin's I.'

'Would that I too, I might borrow
Wings that waft you hence to-morrow,
    Kinsman fair.
Would that I might rise and follow
Over Ocean, under hollow
    Arch of air;
    Flee away and be at rest,
    Heron, in thy happy West.'

COLUMBA.

Go, Ronan, go: my heartstrings are the chords
You play on.

RONAN.

Master, when the bard is gone,
Thy heartstrings will make music of themselves.
Then listen thou. [*Exit.*

COLUMBA.

Gone. But it echoes on,
That music, thrilled against my heart. Perhaps,
Father, thy sign, the omen for my doubt.
Ay, how my soul went with him, as he climbed
Labouringly up the spiring stair of heaven,
Then from that watch-tower summit, saw and shot
Due for his home and mine. O Home and Kin,
Ye first of voices in the dooms of men,
Shall ye not be the last, and I obey?

MOCHONNA *enters.*

MOCHONNA.

All things are ordered for the voyage, sire.
To-morrow ho! for Alba and the Isle.

COLUMBA.

What! *you* so glad, Mochonna!

MOCHONNA.

Why not I?

N

COLUMBA.

Well, well. Your time went blithely. Hands of kin,
Found on your twelve-year parting's hither side,
Have pressed a welcome ; kindly eyes have smiled
On your unfolded manhood. Sit awhile,
Son mine, I have a thought to break to you.

MOCHONNA.

Your son to hear it ever.

COLUMBA.

This it is.
I scarce would have you go with me to Hy.

MOCHONNA.

Father !

COLUMBA.

For I would have your manhood spent
For the loved West and in it.

MOCHONNA.

Not with you ?

COLUMBA.

Why, since I must to Alba, not with me.

MOCHONNA.

I am all astonished at your words and lost.
What should I do in Erin?

COLUMBA.

     Be as I
Was once in Erin; rule my Houses here,
Derry and all her sisters; guard the life
Christ gave us; water where I planted erst;
Keep whole the pure tradition, dower it more.
I charge you not by your obedience now;
But by our fellowship I plead with you
To put the young hand to the plough I left.

MOCHONNA.

But I have put hand to a plough already.
Dare I look back?

COLUMBA.

    No looking back is this,
To drive God's plough across a wealthier field.

MOCHONNA.

Wealthier? My father, can you mean the word?
I know it is a thorny glebe we ear

In Britain, but the soil is virgin.   O
The joy of the new seedland ; hearts untamed,
Our capture ; souls that open to our word
Fresh as the mountain flower to suns of May.
But you that loved the Pict and saved him, prize
That harvest well.

COLUMBA.

That harvest can be reaped
By ruder husbandmen.   There's more to say.
I have marked your way with the fierce chieftains here,
And theirs with you.   I think it shame to blunt
The fine tool's temper on the coarser need.
Nay, wave it not away.   God's gift is God's,
To fear and to revere, but use withal.
And by that birthright charm of nobleness,
And by the sudden fire which kindles on you
Among your peers, I know you framed to sway
Princes, not peasants.

MOCHONNA.

O you little know !
You would not be your own son's tempter else.
There is a wild pulse, that has beat before,
Stirred at your speech.   For once my kin and twice
Have whispered me of power.   They set the lure

Too broadly, they, for then I thought of one
True youth who lost a crown to gain the Christ.
I too would choose as purely, if I may.

COLUMBA.

Ah yes, do I not know it? This way lies
Temptation. Yet for holy cause a man
Must dare be tempted. Son, remember it,
We are debtors to the Gael and to the Briton,
But to our household first. The cause of brothers
Is holy cause, Mochonna.

MOCHONNA.

Holy cause,
Thrice holy. But my brothers—who are they?
There's a tall fisher-lad in far-off Hy
Came to the beach at parting, wrung my hand,
Then kissed it sobbing 'Friend, come quickly home.
The firefit else will take me, and you not here.'
My brothers! All the brother in my heart
Is given to this my brother and to those
My hundred of rude Alba. Part me not,
Chief shepherd, from the flock you gave.

COLUMBA.

Again,
Do not I know? Left I no flock of mine

In Erin? But if God who asked thy self
For the flock's sake, shall now require the flock,
Only that once more He may ask the self,
Harder to give, so given—how answer you?

MOCHONNA.

Why, if God ask——. But no, it is not so.
I know it, but I cannot reason it.
There's a blind something in my being's core
That sees more clear than eyesight, plainlier speaks
Than utterance, 'Break not heaven's unsevered clue:
Keep whole life's sacred line, or forfeit weal:
Fate spins not twice, nor Heaven, the threads of men.'
And my thread is enwoven, sire, with thine,
As thine with Alba's. I will keep it whole:
Go where Columba goes, where bides, abide:
Till he bid sunder. And he has not bidden.

COLUMBA.

Nor will he bid it. Son, we two go on,
We two. Would God I knew but whither! Enough.
Go sit and muse your sweet farewells of Erin,
While I——. I have spoken half my thought, but half:
The rest, when God has given it. Go, my son.

[MOCHONNA *goes.*

'Fate spins not twice, nor Heaven, the threads of men.'

How strong and true and single runs the thread
Of life for him, and shining as it runs,
Not to be missed.   He steers no doubting way.
How otherwise Columba.   O to choose !
My heart and reins are wearying with the toil :
While he but thought upon his fisher-lad
And all was clear.   Sooth, they have cause to love him.
Some day when he is laid away to sleep
On the salt marge with Oran, he will be
Saint of the fishers' love, his glory hymned
In the low chant as laden gunwales bring
The netted spoil at morning ; his the name
Cried from the perilled coracle-side to ban
The sea-beast's monster gambol ; his be cried
When races up the sound the swallowing fog
And blots red Malea and blanched sands of Hy.

> [*A pause.*

But I, this weary while, have yet to choose.

Ah !
Why lo ! 'tis chosen ; and I knew it not.
Nor know I how.   My battling thought had sunk
Like a spent swimmer gulfed in the dark sea.
And then—why, sudden, I was all one light,
And no part dark : from all my being a fire
(As if a sign were scrolled along the sky)

Ran blazoning out on my soul's vision a name,
' Alba.'   The witchery of that counter-scene,
Cloud-glories risen in the alluring West
To daze the o'er-tempted spirit, the pomp, the glow,
The weight and imminence of that pageant high
Drift like a wrecked storm leeward. ,And a peace,
Such peace has fallen as where God showers a dew
Of benediction on the fold of Heaven.

ACT FIFTH.

SCENE I.

The seashore of Iona. Circiter A.D. 590. Columba
alone.

COLUMBA.

Nay, 'tis this memoried night of Whitsuntide
Has vexed me with the dream.   Even yet my heart
Aches with it in this sunshine.   There's a voice
Away from me this while, could charm it hence.

Erin !   To dream again of Erin, and wake,
Tears in my eyes, crying ' I will not go ' :
And as it were a hand upon my breast
Pushing me forth from what I clung to.   Ay,
A dream : a shadow.   But a shadow of what ?
The thing that nears us casts a shadow too.
Would thou wert home, Mochonna.

o

Dream ?   I think,

It is my fate comes up to wrestle me,
Casting the shadow, as yon sea-bird's wing
Comes westward over the grass before him——

Ha !

[*Seeing* MOCHONNA.

Why, how !   What blessed south-wind of the June
Has blown you hither a week before your hour ?

[*Embraces him.*

I think my wish must be the wonder-worker.
Son, I was breathing it e'en now.

MOCHONNA.

Your wish

Has always worked a wonder, father mine,
Yet, scarce so quickly : 'tis a morn and night
Since *my* wish urged a coracle's head to sea.
I had sped.   How could I tarry ?   And the boy
That six long weeks should play Mochonna here,
I fear he played it ill then.

COLUMBA.

Nay, indeed.

Apt scholar is your Diormit ; was yourself
For tender service at the old man's need.

I missed you not, or only——.   Heaven forgive
That I should talk of this, and have not asked
How fared Mochonna's work in Derry.

MOCHONNA.

Well.

Too well.   I was an idle envoy.   Peace
Outran me, and no part was mine to do
But chant *Quam bonum, fratres!* over hands
That clasped again without me.

COLUMBA.

Ay and ay.

Were they so speedy, son?   But I have heard
The wrinkled ice-brook snap his chain an hour
Ere the kind South came talking in the glen;
And yet the South wind was the Spring.   What else?
Saw you good Fergus, and what said he?

MOCHONNA.

Truth,

He shook a silvered forelock, and he growled,
As some old war-dog grinding a worn fang,
'Grey am I, but no wiser now than then.
I told him truth.   He should have stayed.'   But there
He gripped me strongly, 'Tell your prince of priests,

Since he'll not fight for me, why let him pray
For his poor fighting Fergus.　Yea, and tell him,
I love him now as then,'—so turned and went.
There passed no more between us.

COLUMBA.

And your kin—
Still would they have Mochonna home ?

MOCHONNA.

O sire,
Wrong not your son !　Forget them.

COLUMBA.

Ay, forget.
How easily !　So far away and dead
That old fear of a severing doom, until
This grey age whiten to an end.　O son,
How gladsome is this morn of Pentecost
That blows you home long sighed for !　Warmer for it
The sunshine wraps my aging limbs, the blooms
Of our spare coverts open, as we talk,
Wider and whiter, and their scanty choir
Pipe boldlier than I knew them.

MOCHONNA.

'Tis the Spring,
Father, in your own veins.　May age to me

Come as to you, who know of winter's frost
Nought but the rime amidst your hair.

COLUMBA.

To you ?
Age come to you, Mochonna ? Never will it.
Yours is a youth that keeps my age from me,
And old I cannot image you.

Alack !
[Seeing a Pictish messenger approach.
Here's one to part us, or I read amiss
The signs of envoy. Be not far away
The while I hear him.

[Goes apart with the messenger.

MOCHONNA (pacing alone).

'Part us ?' Part.—Is that
A cloud that crossed the sunlight ? Nay, the sky
Is stainless. 'Twas a numbness of the long,
Chill seas that left me with a shiver. How glad
Shone the grey eyes on me, so deep, so pure,
As our pure deeps that breathe the sunlight down,
Alive and lucent to their agate floor !
And they could think that I would leave him ! Well,
At last 'tis over : they'll not tempt me more.
We twain go on together, till the end.

And then—and then——. What will Mochonna then ?
> [*Pauses at the edge of a hollow.*

Ha ! Why, 'tis good the hermit is from home :
He had heard me. I have stumbled on the cell
Of Ernan, where he plays the anchorite,
This hollow, rounded as a mavis' nest,
A whimsy of the winds that whirl or heap
Our shifting sands to shape and shape again
The island meadow. Here he sits and sees
The round bowl under, the round heaven above,
Lifted as in a cup to starland. Ah !
For him 'tis well. Yet I——. 'Twas earnest there
With yon wild stranger. He has sped. They part.
> [*Rejoins* COLUMBA.

His errand is soon ended, sire.

COLUMBA.

> He brought

A message from the East. His tribesmen crave
A preacher from the island.

MOCHONNA.

> And the hive

Can spare them him. We are full forced. I know
Ten that would answer at your lifted hand.

COLUMBA.

I do believe it.   But this folk is bold:
'Send us your best,' they ask me, 'send your best.'
Well, I will send—whom I will send.   Enough.
Back to our talk.   You have not told a word
Of the leal House of Durrow.

MOCHONNA (*abstractedly*).

All was well,

Far as I heard.

COLUMBA.

And they have filled their ranks
After the sickness ?

MOCHONNA.

As I think.

COLUMBA.

The King

Holds by his promise ?

MOCHONNA.

Yea, he holds, they said.

COLUMBA.

(*Aside.*)   What ails him then?   (*Aloud.*) Saw you not
   Ernan there?

MOCHONNA.

Ernan!

COLUMBA.

He surely sent his word to me.

MOCHONNA.

Was he not here in Britain?

COLUMBA.

                 Dreaming! son.
We speak of Irish Ernan,—but your thoughts
Wander—the tongue-bound, blighted child whom I
(The simpler take it half for miracle)
Loosed from his dismal chain.   And strange it was
How the smit branch outblossomed.

MOCHONNA.

                   Yes, I saw—
My thoughts had strayed—I know not what—forgive.
Full sure I saw your Ernan, if the straight
And gainly youth I saw be surely he.

Free speech is his, free wits. They whisper him
The preacher of some decade hence ; so well
You wrought with him.   O he forgets it not !
For talking of you at the board I felt
A gaze that burned on me, and, glancing, caught
His eyes aflame consuming me.   They dipped
Lids on a reddening cheek.   And when I pressed
To bear his message home, the graceful speech,
Tongue-fast as with the old infirmity,
Could only falter, ' Tell him that I pray
Never to shame him.'   Yet 'twill please you, so.

COLUMBA.

Dear child ! and said he so ?   Heaven's dews be on him !
Ah ! son, the bud which had not opened, save
For our poor tendance, is the flower we love.
There's one life more on barren earth for us.

MOCHONNA (*abruptly*).

Father, if you should live three lives of man
There still would be a youth, when I am gone,
To love, as I have loved you.

COLUMBA.

                    Son, what words !
When you are gone ! So you would from me.

P

MOCHONNA.

Would!

Ay, when Mochonna's loves are turned to hates,
And all the holy past a thing unclean,
Then would I, then; no sooner. Sire, what words!

COLUMBA.

There is no wrong in them. An hour of God
Calls whom it will, not when they will, nor whither.
I meant no more, true son. Away with this.
Come now your counsel in this question risen,
Whom I should send to the eastward folk, a flock
That asks a wise hand and a fearless too;
Fierce and with neighbours fiercer. Fruit the more
For who can shepherd them. Shall Ernan go?

MOCHONNA.

None braver. Yet those hermit winters cramp
Somewhat the free mind's sinew. He that goes
Lither must be, and apt for change and chance.
Say rather Fechno.

COLUMBA.

Yet I doubt him here.
This shepherd must be ruler too, and he—

Heaven pardon if my thoughts are earthly—yet
The princely blood for ruling.

MOCHONNA.

                       Is the work
(I fear almost to ask), but is it worth
Our Baithen's venture ?

COLUMBA.

                   Worth ! what is it not ?
The stark East's capture ; Britain, sea to sea,
One fold of Christ's. What were too costly ? Yet
Too well he rules in Ethica. Withal
Baithen's strong years are done. It is not he.
Strength must be his and time to work his will
Who ventures thither.

MOCHONNA.

            Youth is plenty with us ;
Lugneius, Mocumin, and Fintan.

COLUMBA.

                    Boys.
I may not squander their unhardened prime
In wars beyond them. Nay, but name no more.
This choice will tax us : let it rest. I think

God will provide Himself—a priest, my son.

But go you now within and greet the House,
For fear they grudge me; then re-weave our talk
With bosoms freer of this care.   Farewell.

MOCHONNA.

Farewell?   Why even but now it was Good-morrow.

COLUMBA.

And yet farewell; and take the father's kiss
Going.   I fear to lose you one short hour
Now, who have lost you late so many and long.
Farewell.   The peace of Heaven be with thee, son.

MOCHONNA.

And with thy spirit, father.

[Goes.

COLUMBA.

Peace with me !—
Did he discern ?—A cloud there fell on him:
Strayed thoughts: a stumbling speech.   And how we
     swerved
Suddenly from the touch, as fishing barks
Drift in the blind haze on a consort's beam,
Then glimpse and shudder asunder ere they jar !
'Send us your best.'   And wherefore ?   Bold are they.

Yet 'tis a great door that is opened, great.
I dare not say them nay.   But then ' my best.'
Why, that is he, none other.   Him I cannot:
Son of my spirit, grown my brother.   No.
There is some other, best for this; not he:
Some other, though 'twere Baithen's self.   Alas!
God is not mocked, and He will have the best.
And like a river His Will enfolding mine
Sweeps it along, still clutching this and that,
Still borne unstayed beyond them, and the fall
Booms in my ears.   Kind God, be pitiful.
Since what Thou askest I must give it, Thou
Ask me not this, ask not my half of life;
My faith's true Angel; saint whose lamp, unblown
By any gust of earth, uplighted mine
At the awful crossways.   Lighted—ah! for what?
I rendered power for love, must love for love
Be rendered last?   Son, art thou grown to be
Dread Angel of the Passion, ministering
A cup we drink together, lip with lip?
Yea, stern the Christ is and will have no less;
But sends this lonely, lonelier age to pace
The last, sad miles friendless, a single soul,
When need of friend is sorest.   Christ, I bow;
I draw this wine of wormwood to my lips,
If he—we drink not or we drink together—

If he—for must I bid him ?   O my soul,
What if Mochonna wills not ?   Wise is he:
Sudden, but wise in suddenness; the Spirit
Deals with him by the lightning.   Lo, I'll trust
His heart's word, as an angel's cry from heaven
Staying the doom before it fall.   O yet
God will provide Himself an offering, son !

[Goes.

RONAN *enters and crosses, singing.*

O a bark and forth to the silent North,
    Never a mate with me,
To steer her fair for isles of prayer
    In a land where no men be,
For the rocks that meet the angel feet
    Flown over the sail-less sea.

Though, sooth, I know not if they find the Christ
Nearer, who go so far to seek Him.   Well:
Harp, lie you safe the while I fetch the gear.

[Lays his harp in a coracle, and goes.

MOCHONNA *enters.*

MOCHONNA.

Gone.   Well, I sought him not.   I meant to 'scape
The household bounds, and breathe the air.   A mood
Of restlessness is on me; and 'tis strange,

Seeing I longed but now for rest and home.
Kind too they were in welcome. But the Pict,
How his eyes followed me! They drove me out,
They or a something in his tale. He moved
To stay me passing, but I would not see.
I am half sorry that I would not. Well,
This choice will tax the House.

      What's here? The harp
Of Ronan in a tethered coracle's prow.
He will be faring o'er the sound anon.
I'll wait him here.

     'Baithen's strong years are done.'
Else he had spared him for't; and that is much,
He needing helpers in this ebb of life.
Had this but fallen sooner, had it fallen
Some later day——. Yet Diormit loves him well,
And haply—fie upon my thoughts. Their need
Is great, his own is greater.

      Ronan tarries;
And fast the tide flows out from Hy. The bark
Totters half beached, half in the jostling wave.
I'll push it seaward. So. What trick is this
The quick mind played? I thought of Galilee,
And a forth-faring bark and one who cried
'Lord, let me first go lay in earth my sire.'
Stayed he or followed? For they told us not.

I am grown strangely sad.　Come quicklier you,
Kind minstrel.　Yet there's somewhat at my heart
Would bid me be alone.　Why, let me muse,
While Ronan stays, my counsel in this strait;
It will be asked ere sunset.　Nay, 'tis spent.
New way there is not, and new name is none.
And yet what fitter chance for who were fit;
When will the slow moons bring another as fair?
Myself, if this were mine———.　But peace, my soul,
Thine is it not.

　　　　　　　　Yet home is hard to leave.
Poor Drostan of our Convent of the Tears,—
The years have dried that storm upon his cheek
Long since, but how he wept the while, and how
Clung to Columba's hand, sobbing his prayer
Not to be sundered from him, not to bide
Sole in the friendless wild.　We wept with him,
And named it from our tears.　Poor Drostan!　I,
Should I be hardier-hearted?　Peace, my soul;
It calls not thee———

　　　RONAN (*entering at the other side of the boat*).
　　　　　　　Sir, would you o'er the sound?

　　　MOCHONNA.

Ha, Ronan!　Stolen on me from behind!

And I so looking for you.   Yes, the sound.
Let us go o'er.   And, Ronan, sing the while.
Your sail will speed us east without the oar.

> [*They enter the boat.*

RONAN.

Old songs or new, which will you ?

MOCHONNA.

> Nay, the old :

The oldest, one you made beneath the oak
Of Derry, till you spied me watching you,
And broke your strain.   I never heard the end.

RONAN.

I care not for it.   Choose some other one.

MOCHONNA.

But I care, Ronan : and I choose none else.

RONAN.

Why, then——.   (*Aside*).   I would he had not asked me this.
    (*Sings.*)
        What was that ye saw, my son, and started,
                Changing cheer ?
        What is this ye strain so long with parted
                Lips to hear ?

' 'Tis the war-horn on the wind, my father, calling :
    'Tis the war-horn on the wind.'

Let it blow, my son, so strong and many
    Troops the glen :
Leave not you the old man's side for any
    Call of men.
' Who should lead them but the chief's son, O my
    father :
    Who should lead them for the chief ? '

Nay, but keep thee in the fence beside me,
    Soldier son :
Keep thee fast, for, if the death betide thee,
    Chief is none.
' Sire, the chieftain for the vanward not the shelter,
    When the war-horn's on the wind.'

You pierce me with those eyes ! What ails you, sir ?
Forbear. I cannot end it.

MOCHONNA.

           Ended is it.
Ronan shall sing Mochonna song no more.
I heard the voices of all sires of mine
Sound on thy strings : and all their hands are laid

To draw me where I would not and I would.
Set me on shore, dear minstrel, for I go.

RONAN.

O sir, and whither?

MOCHONNA.

To the battle front.
Old warrior comrade, you have sung me thither.
Go tell Columba I have broken pale
Third time and last; for, if his best were I,
Then is the best gone eastward.   Say to him
He wills it, though he knows it not; and I
Not will, but know it: and I come no more,
Except he bids me,——and he will not bid.

[*Goes.*   RONAN *gazes after him, then seizes
his harp and sings.*

Why is this ye come from warward trooping,
    Soldiers true?
Who is this lies under banners drooping,
    Borne of you?
'He who fell at battle's edge, and o'er him fallen
    Swept his clansmen as the storm.'

SCENE II.

Iona.   The Abbot's hut.   A.D. 597.

DIORMIT (*without, at the door*).

My father, shall I enter ?

COLUMBA.

          Yea, my son.

What hinders my Mochonna ?

DIORMIT.

          Father !

COLUMBA.

                Ah !

Forgive me, dear son Diormit, the old brain
Was dreaming still.   What would you with me, son ?

DIORMIT.

Baithen is come.   You called upon him twice,
When the trance lifted yester-eve.   But then
Again it fell.   You heard not when at night
Softly we called your name.   We dared no more,
Because of the strange light which hardly yet

Had faded from the crannies.   But he waits,
Baithen—if you will speak with him.

COLUMBA.

Yea, yea.
Too late he comes, yet send him.

[DIORMIT *goes.*

Christ, my hope,
I thought Thy day had dawned on me, but lo!
The grey, grey lift o'er Malea.   Watches yet
For Thy worn sentinel, who can but watch,
Lamed with his seventy years and seven of march.
But the end nears me.

[BAITHEN *enters.*

Baithen, come at last!
Ah! but too late.

BAITHEN.

Late?   As I might, I came:
No later.   The great wind has held me bound.
What need of me the while: what chance has fallen?

COLUMBA.

Things beyond words, and thoughts above my thought,
Thou couldst have heard.   Why wert thou from my side?

BAITHEN.

How ! Heard you not nor felt with what a wind
Earth groaned and ocean laboured these three days ?

COLUMBA.

Wind ? Yea, my son, a rushing mighty wind
I heard : but ocean heard it not nor earth.
A rushing mighty wind, and in the wind
A voice that spake with me such things as thou——.
Why wast thou from me, Baithen ?

BAITHEN.

Blame me not.
To Egga's shore, my errand done, I came,
Drawn by I knew not what that yearned within,
To ship for Hy and thee. But 'twixt us stood
An ever-toppling, ever-mounting wall
Prisoning our craft upon the beach. A day
I watched the waves : but then the yearning grew
Past bearing, till I pushed my men aboard,
Because a moment's quiet eased the deep,
But had not cleared the harbour horn, when down
Swooped the quick tempest's wing, and caught the bark,
Half from the giddy wave-top lifted her,
And tossed her back like a leaf to the shrieking shore.

COLUMBA.

I wronged thee. Pardon it. But sore it was,
When the sweet vision's chain had loosed awhile
This three-days' prisoner of the Lord, to miss
My Baithen. Thou art nearest me: thy faith
A wave that ever surely climbed with mine,
Slowlier, and sank not with it, but remained
To mark where both had mounted. 'Twas for thee,
Hadst thou been here to hearken. In thine ear
A word had been a thousand.

BAITHEN.

              I am here
At last, my father: shall I hear it?

COLUMBA.

                Nay.
When first I looked abroad, a rainbow lit
His beacon over Malea's brow: the sun
Dipped: 'twas a blind wrack on a dead sea-crag.
God's spirit was the sun, my soul the cloud:
I burned and I am dark.

BAITHEN.

          No memory, none?

Tarrying before your door our Diormit heard
A voice (and hardly knew it yours) that rose
Chanting; and words he caught, but mystic all
And past his wit, he said, to render them.
Has the song died and left no echo?

COLUMBA.

None
That I can voice to others, even to thee.
For, if I sang, 'twas in some bound of heaven,
Where blew the wind of heaven and swept a strain
From mortal harp-strings. And it blows not here.

BAITHEN.

Strange! For what profit in a vision given
And gone,—a moment's shadow on a stream
That glasses and forgets it? Barren grace
Were this, my master.

COLUMBA.

Nay, for I have seen.
I looked on heights and depths, I heard the words
That make the great worlds and the soul of man.
But in the spirit I heard, and in the spirit
I shall remember.

BAITHEN.

Yet from all the tract
Of those tranced days and nights does no word live ?
No drift or salvage of one dream escape
The engulfing silence ?   We would treasure it,
As 'twere an angel's message.

COLUMBA.

Would ye so ?
Why, there is one dream I recall, but one ;
First dreamt, alone remembered, 'gainst the wont
Of dreamers.   Sooth ! no angel's message is it.
A brother's all too human tale.   But hear it.
   That morn before my trance I sat and wrote
Awhile in David, but at *Quoniam*
Defecit in dolore vita mea,
Et anni mei—stayed, and loosed the pen
(So soon the old hand tires), and looked abroad.
Bleak in the slow spring lay our tiny glebe,
And bleak and near gaunt Malea, ribbed with snow.
A sudden hunger gnawed my heart: I thought
How the merle tunes his music on the lawns
Of our loved Erin, and from somewhere came
A searing whisper, 'Was it lost for this ?
And has the white beard sped so well ?'   And then

R

At once the whole long island sojourn seemed
As empty as a faded afternoon.
And was it I, or the near demon, mocked
Our toils in Alba, 'here and there a rood
Planted; a shepherd, and a score of sheep:
And here a mountain chief half-tamed; and there
On rock or promontory a hermit left
(Lone as the ice bear on his travelling float
That topples him at last) to muse and pray
Seven years, and starve and pass.'   O Baithen, then
For a moment, for a rebel moment rose,
What slept in me, not died, my nature's sin,
World's-pride, though faint, as in an old man's veins,
World's-pride, an ebbing, hungry, helpless sea
That crawls and mutters at the dead shore-foot,
And upward looks to where his vehement arms
Made throb the deep cliff and the panting caves
With transports of his strength.   O Baithen, thou
Of constant souls most constant, sidesman true
On whose unshaken shoulder leant my strength
Oft in faint pause of war, thou'lt not believe
The tamed earth-lust could rise and wrestle and shake
The foothold of the immortal hope with doubt
Lest all were vanity: 'Fools of Heaven,' it hissed,
'Who sell true earth-gold for the golden cloud,
The good which shall not be.'   Believe it not,

Brother: for this was dreaming, that which fell
Thereafter was the waking.   For to earth,
As one who, swooning at the precipice-edge,
Clutches the safe sward's bosom, prone I fell,
Shuddering, and dumbly prayed the living Christ
Smite the doubt-demon o'er my cowering head.
And then—I cannot tell what happened then,
Nor if a moment passed me or an hour,
Or what of me it was that walked at large
Over an island plain 'twixt sea and sea,
Like to thy Ethica.   One sat to weave
Beside a rush-bed: patiently he wove
And wove: I marked a smile that rippling made
Doubtful the lines of sorrow on his cheek,
And standing o'er him asked, 'What gladdens you,
Who seem so lone?'   And he, as if no man,
But his sole thought had spoken, 'Who so glad
As he who loves much, being much forgiven?'
'Hast thou found peace,' I said, 'my Libran?'   He
Turned dreaming-wise, and suddenly saw, and then
—O how to tell thee what a gaze of love
(My heart as at a fire was molten at it)
Clasped me about! 'Part me no more,' he cried,
'No more, great father,' and he reached a hand. -
But, ere it touched, I was away, away.

Yet arms there were on me, I thought, but slim

And childish, and down rippled to my lap
Gold hair of Aidan's Hector.   Aidan's self
Stooped to my shoulder, kissed the fair boy's brow
Half hidden there, and 'Man of God, thou sayest:'
He murmured, 'Yea, the anointed of the Lord,
By sign of who best loves our noblest.   He
Shall pay thee for the sire.'
                                    But there his voice
Changed to far off, and stern from tender.   Helmed
Stood Aidan: on his brand the sinking moon:
And 'Fear not,' came the word, 'my soldiers: clear
Across the night I heard Columba's prayer.
He strikes on our side from the isle of Christ:
He, whom Christ loveth, loves us.'   And thereat
A thousand faces glanced the moon, with eyes
Lit from a fire not hers.
                                    But when I thought
To hear against their breasts the heathen wave
Roaring, behold! no heathen host, but one
Grey weary chieftain, coming, propped of twain,
From a skiff's side towards me, as I sat
Under Skye's pinnacles in a reddening eve.
'I, Raven of the Rock, am come to thee,
The Dove of Erin, for thou knowest Him
Whom I, not knowing, all a life have sought.
Give me the holy water, swear me His,

That I may be His man before I pass
To-morrow.'   I wept, so shone in those worn eyes
The faith Christ lights unknown, without the word.
And eastward climbed the grey sail up the seas,
And on their summit flamed, as if a soul
Blossomed in fire and mounted.

                       Here a voice
Turned me.   A man knelt by me, cowled as we,
Thick snows upon the cowl.   For now the air
Was blind with snow, and nothing else I saw
But a great tabled stone, pillared on twain,
The wild man's altar: over it a cross
Glimmered, through drift.   I raised the head.   Ah me!
Dallan! who went not with us to the work:
Dallan! who after went, men said, to Alba,
But none knew whither.   Pale he looked me o'er,
Not shamed, with eyes that searched me, till I spake,
'How fare you, brother?'   Then he clutched my robe,
'Yea, yea! for brother I am, not traitor now:
Brother.   I seek a lost sheep o'er the hills,
And die in the storm.   Christ seek him!   Thou, my sire,
Fear not to bless me.   I have risen who fell.
Thy sorrowing eyes so wrought in me, I vowed,
Because I went not, I would further go
Than who went furthest.   And I kept it hid,
That Christ alone on my unworthiness

Might look and less despise me.   See, He wills
The master whom I wronged should look on me
And not despise me.'   On my breast he lay.
The white scud wrapped us eddying.   Heart to heart
We drank the joy of parted souls at one,
In silence, curtained by the wandering storm.

BAITHEN.

Dallan !   Pray heaven the truth be as the dream,
For thou art prophet.   And it ended so ?

COLUMBA.

Ah ! no : not so it ended, friend : not so   .   .   .
A moment suffer me   .   .   .   I will speak auon.

BAITHEN.

Nay, then, let be, my father.   Other time,
If this time pains, will serve us.

COLUMBA.

                              Baithen, stay.
No other time.   Come near me : seat you close.
Here, at my side ; and lay your hand in mine.
Ah ! you remember now,—that night—the three,
Who stemmed a stream together, hand in hand,

Through the dread, holy dark.   They are not loosed,
Those hands: for listen.

                    When the vision's wing
Swept with me onward, 'twas as if I waked,
So clearer was the dream than other dreams,
So all the senses lived in it together,
Undreamlike, nor I heard alone and saw,
But felt the ruffling air, the prick of cold,
The moorland savours.   Dark against the dawn
A shrine rose on a naked promontory.
I neared: the door was wide, and round it stood,
In-gazing, fingering edge of axe and brand,
A hundred wolfish men, like wolves afret
Nosing a sheep-door.   Yet I passed them through.
A priest bent o'er the chalice: right and left,
Six brethren on a side, his Household knelt,
Nor at the darkening door uplooked.   The priest
Rose upright.   By the princely head I knew,
O Baithen, our Mochonna.   But he turned,
To part with those doomed twelve the awful cup,
And scarce I knew,—such sternly-tender change
On lips and eyes the coming passion wrought.
But me he called not to the feast, nor saw.
Then when they rose and chanted, on their brows
Death's shadow was not shadow but a fire,
From inward breathed, as if God's finger there

Lit the white lamp that dies not.   But for me,
My veins with helpless wrath beat in my head
And pity for the slain and slayer, the sheep
Wolf-fanged to rend the shepherd.   He the while
All in a low clear voice untremblingly
Praying the peace of God, upcast his eyes
To where dawn's golden arrow smote the spark
High in the rafter : then he brought them down
Full over me, and still he saw me not :
But spake, ' O brothers tried, dear Company
Of the Red Martyrdom, as Christ has willed,
We die : and we have wrought no deed and no
Deliverance on the earth ; and there will be
No name of us nor memory, save in these
Wild hearts that slay unknowing, who shall come
Through love of whom they slew to love of Him
For whom we die.   Let us go hence, my friends.
And this one last time follow me.'   He moved,
As if none stood between him and the swords.
' Will he not know me ? ' groaned my heart.   He heard,
He looked—O with a look as if I stood
With still the severing mountain leagues between
—And said without the lips, ' Yea, yea, and thou,
With whom I die not, father—till white age
Join whom the red death sunders, O farewell ! '
But there he caught his breath, for he had seen.

O there was never touch between us, eyes
Only, as spirit enfolds a spirit, close
Beyond all earth's embraces folded us
One age-long moment in the strain of love !
And joying I let pass to death my son.

My vision blinked and glimpsed again.   A crowd
Made tumult ; from the heart of it there came
A something, and a hand that closed on mine,
Viewless, with power, and drew me with it afar,
Yea, to the unimaginable afar,
Where the worlds are not, and the shining stair
Climbs to the timeless Presence : and there befell
What the soul locks within nor looks on more
This side the shadowy threshold.   Yet in all
The glory of Heaven's golden overspill
One joy was master, and one strain in all
Her songs was burden and a beating heart :
For how that music spoke in blessed ears
I know not, but in mine it chanted still,
'There lives no glory but the living Love :
On earth the sowing and the flower above :
For Love the deed is and the meed is Love.'

O Baithen, and my deed on earth is done,
Some deed by me unworthy—I have loved.

S

And here have known the meed; but elsewhere soon
Shall know, Christ willing, for my steps are nigh
The shadowy threshold of the shining stair,
Not backward to be crossed again.   But you,
Who must rule after me, remember—nay,
How should I counsel one in whom our House
Such likeness of Love's own apostle finds ?
Yet, for I bought this knowledge at a price,
Fortune and home and fame and lust of will,
Hear it.   No deed can live but only Love's :
No might of man nor fierceness, nor the craft
Of kingly nature, nor the seated will,
But one strong Spirit that not seeks her own.
Love therefore ye.   There is no deed but love.

BAITHEN.

I cannot answer thee.   This coming hour
Will orphan us in very truth.   Go forth
Our glory.   I will tarry, as I may.

SCENE III.

The shore of Iona.   A great wind blowing.   RONAN *alone.*

RONAN (*sings*).

Bluster and buffet thy fill,
    Loud wind of the west ;
Wrangle and wrestle at will
    Thy maddest, thy best,
Till the shaken sea cup overspill
    On the far meadow's breast,
And with yeasty wave bubble the hill
    And with foam flower is drest.
Blow wind, and blow ever, nor cease :
The storm to the minstrel is peace.

A day and a day and a day,
    And ever the blast ;
A blast that hath rapt from his clay
    Our strong one at last.
Blow wind, for thy tumults upstay,
    With her weeping held fast,
My heart, as a cloud on its way
    With its waters uncast.
She is borne, as a cloud, in the rush,
She will break, as the cloud, in the hush.

Why do we sing, my harp? He's gone we sang for,
Sailing the great wind with his angel-guard
To the house of God. I should have snapped thy strings
Or given thee burial in the dumb sea-bed.

    For the holy Isle's dark
      And her glory gone past her:
    The harp hath no mark,
      Nor the minstrel a master.

Buried thee? Yea, and followed thee. But he
Hinders: the dead hand holds me: he that tamed
The wild man out of Ronan, master still.
'Live thou thy life, bard: Christ would have thee sing,'
He told me once. Half heathen again am I,
Missing him. Yet he holds me.
        [*To* DIORMIT, *who comes round the rocks.*
                Ah! fair brother.
What seek you?

         DIORMIT.

      Wilful Ronan, whom but you?
You only from the burial, you alone!
Why, from his stall old Whitefrock followed us
Stumbling in rear to watch him laid in earth,
And weeping manlike tears as when he dropped
His head in the Abbot's lap that last of morns.
His Bard to fail him, and no creature else!

RONAN·(*pointing*).

Diormit, what make the folk that cluster there
Thick on the dunes beyond the strait?

DIORMIT.

Belike

They watched the burial train.

RONAN.

How knew they of it?

None passed such water of death to learn the news.

DIORMIT.

Nay, but old Aedh, that morrow of our grief,
Shot over on the vanward of the gale,
Swift as our wing-clipped raven, when a gust
Caught him on Duni's height and blew him away
To the far fisher's door.   Aedh bides with them:
The poor lame bird had winged as easily back.
But wherefore, Ronan, wherefore you away?

RONAN.

I will not tell thee, boy.   Nay, frown not you.
I love you well, fair Diormit; and your years
Are now as Ronan's own when first he loved
Ronan's lost lord and Diormit's.   Bear with me.
I will not tell, because I cannot tell.

Yet, when the gale's rude trumpet suffers me
(As even now it blows a lessening note),
Perchance I'll tell the seas and all the stars.
Whom should I else?   They are his kinsmen, they;
For he is brother of the star's white truth
And the sea's stormy glory.   Let me be:
Go, gentle friend: we are well paired in sorrow,
But I must mourn him in my kind alone.

DIORMIT.

Well, you shall tell it to your stars and seas.
But they'll forget it all.   So would not I,
When you will trust me with it, as we sit
Upon the warm lee of the Angel Knoll,
And watch the nearing sea-birds hover and pause,
Marking us, like the white-winged messengers
Seeking the master's soul four summers since,
Whom our prayer turned to heaven again.   Alas!
We could not turn them twice.   Live, Ronan, you:
Who keeps the great days with us, if you go?

[Goes.

RONAN (sings).

Harp of glory,
Harp of woe,
Magic bride to Ronan's hand troth-plighted
Once in magic youth and long ago,

Minstrel side by side,
Sung have we, O bride,
Field and air and wave in changing story:
Sung the morning's birth,
Sung the eastern hearth
Showering embers live on oakwood hoary.
On thy string was heard
Pipe of waking bird,
Throstle's heart-burst and the cushat's moan:
Sighed the vexed wind through thee,
Sobbed the low brook to thee
What to secret woods he told alone.
Then with chanting higher
Pealed we, harp of fire,
Loud on bounding chords the might of man:
Down thy rhythmic clash
Roared the onset crash,
Leapt thy wild breast under Ronan's span:
Hot the madness sprung,
While on air we flung
Fame of chief and warrior's faith unblamed:
Hand to harp, amain,
Harp to hand again
Tossed the fire and caught the fire and flamed.

Who was this had stolen upon our singing,
    As on sunshine revel steals a cloud ?
Awe was on us, and the strong, upspringing
    Music faltered from her purpose proud.

Failed the glamour from our oakwoods haunted,
    Rose such holier dreamland haunted more ;
Paled the glory from the deeds we vaunted,
    Here was greater than our kings of yore.

Songmate, him we sang not. Ah ! what ailed thee,
    Silent never else when hero passed ?
Silent wert thou, and thy minstrel failed thee
    Numb as charmèd dreamer prison-fast.

Loved we not ? O Christ, but hadst Thou given
    Death for love's sake at the heathen's door,
Heart of Ronan by the doom-spear riven
    Blithe for love had spilt its songful store.

Could love sing ! But here was Love beyond her,
    Love's high sister of the starry wing.
Stooped that dove-wing earthward. We the wonder
    Saw and worshipped, but we might not sing.

Shall we mourn him,
Harp of fame,
Mourn as they who laid him with the worm?
Nay, for we across the blind night's roaring
Heard the beat of eagle vans upsoaring;
Heard, and knew our Strong One rode the storm.
Sing we glory for the deedful spirit
Homeward scaling,
Whence he sways us, and his deeds inherit
Rule unfailing;
Glory for the prince who pride's dominion
Gave for love's;
Yea, the valiant who the eagle's pinion
Changed for dove's.
Who are these who rise and hail him father,
Soldier-sons, and all the lands ingather,
Isle and island, height and highland, shore and shore?
'Neath the shade of our great spirit parted,
Mightier shadow of the mighty-hearted,
Strives a seed and lives a deed for evermore.

THE END.

PRINTED BY WILLIAM BLACKWOOD AND SONS.

www.ingramcontent.com/pod-product-compliance
Lightning Source LLC
Chambersburg PA
CBHW031120020726

47495CB00007B/2276